Praise for *Remember to Forget Me*

"When you step into a story by Kerry Neville, expect to walk into the depths of life. She has the ability to look inside a person and discover the essence of their humanity, no matter how uncomfortable their truth might be. Her prose is so vivid and compelling, and holds such honesty and verve, that you never question where she takes you. You just want to keep walking with her—to find out more about the yearnings that make us who we are." — **Grant Faulkner**, Executive Director of National Novel Writing Month and co-founder of 100 Word Story

"I've long been a fan of Kerry Neville's writing, her shapely sentences and paragraphs, her characters' emotional complexities and the fearless loop-de-loops in her narrative arcs. But in these stories she brings a hard won and singular wisdom to the page, a gravity and elegance that makes the stories linger in my mind long after the significant pleasure of reading them is done." — **Pam Houston**, author of *Contents May Have Shifted*

"Kerry Neville writes with a restless, questing intelligence, creating characters who are never satisfied with the given. They're not afraid of asking themselves the toughest questions if only to keep alive and awake, open to the option of a different way out. The stories in *Remember to Forget Me* linger in the imagination with cinematic power, searing the brain like dreams." — **Paul Lisicky**, author of *The Narrow Door: A Memoir of Friendship*

"In these beautiful stories Kerry Neville moves effortlessly between young and old, Europe and America, always with passion, empathy and marvellous intelligence. Her vivid characters do not give up on love, despite distance, age and indignity. *Remember To Forget Me* is a wonderful and deeply rewarding collection." — **Margot Livesey**, author of *Mercury* and *The Hidden Machinery: Essays on Writing*

Remember to Forget Me

Remember to Forget Me

Stories
by Kerry Neville

BRADDOCK
AVENUE
BOOKS
UNCOMMON BOOKS · UNCOMMON READERS

Printed in the United States of America
10 9 8 7 6 5 4 3 2 1

FIRST EDITION, October 2017

ISBN 10: 0-9989667-3-1
ISBN 13: 978-0-9989667-3-1

The stories in this collection were originally published as follows: "Careless" and "Remember To Forget Me" in *Arts and Letters*; "Home Burial," "Humiliation in Parts," "Survival of the Fittest," and "Zorya," in *Epoch*; "Indignity" and "The Lionman," in *The Gettysburg Review*; and "The Assassin of Bucharest," in *TriQuarterly*.

Cover design by Michelle Bakken Whitaker
Book design by Savannah Adams

Alleyway Books
an imprint of
Braddock Avenue Books
P.O. Box 502
Braddock, PA 15104

www.braddockavenuebooks.com

Braddock Avenue Books is distributed by Small Press Distribution.

For Sophia and Alexander

Contents

"Take me as a relic from the mansion of sorrow;
Take me as a verse from my tragedy;
Take me as a toy, a brick from the house
So that our children will remember to return."
  –Mahmoud Darwish, "A Lover from Palestine"

Remember to Forget Me

stories

Indignity

Every time Maria bathes Mrs. Meinholz, she cannot help but make the comparison: it wasn't like this for her husband Jan, not in the end, not when it was necessary.

"Necessary for what?" her sister Kasia had demanded last week over the telephone.

"To make it easier on him," she said, knowing already this was the wrong thing to say. Kasia never had it easy, took her blows squarely in the face, and moved on.

Then the mute pause of the time delay, two seconds filled with her sister's censure, disappointment, derision, but was only the usual terrible connection to Łęczna.

Kasia's voice cut back in. "To pretend Jan wasn't dying? Or that you couldn't make the dying easier?"

"Just not so exposed." What she meant: instead of the long, windowless shared ward with the mustard-colored, cinder-block walls, his own room at the Wilanow General Clinic, a small one, with a sink that ran both hot and cold water at once, and a tall window that opened out into the branches of a cherry tree thick with pink blossoms and bees. Sheets bleached white. Silence.

"Be grateful it was quick. Move on. You're in America. Don't waste your chance," Kasia said, in reprimand. "All those lonely, fat bachelors with their giant televisions and sports cars and tiny pink dicks. Find one who will give you his credit card and tell you to buy yourself the things that will make you happy. Maybe you will have to fuck him once a week. Maybe suck him once a month. But you will be okay otherwise." Her sister believed Maria's certificate from the six-month Home Health Aide course meant much more than twelve dollars an hour.

She shouldn't have expected sympathy. After all, even when the bruises on Kasia's face could no longer be explained away by a clumsy fall down the stairs, a cabinet opened without thought, a misdirected tennis ball thrown to an incompetent, imaginary dog, Kasia had shrugged off her concern, saying, "We all have to live with something."

Jan always thought Kasia was shallow and calculating, without proper feeling, but, Maria would tell him, this is only because her sister has been without love for so long. Years ago, Kasia had signed up to be a mail-order bride. No matter that she was already married to Ludwik, the fat brute. Kasia could leave her husband behind in Poland to his vodka; he could punch holes into the walls instead of into her. No one would ever know. She showed Maria her photograph in the catalogue. Garish pancake make-up, cheap black bustier over a red lace bra. Next to the other girls, Kasia, already thirty-four, missing two teeth, and trying too hard to look young, was obviously too old. The others? Eighteen and nineteen with slim bodies, lustrous hair, and gentle mouths. They would always be chosen first and there would always be replacements which meant Kasia was never called, never sent to Arkansas or North Dakota, never wanted, even by the perverts.

But Maria? No excuse for this hardening of her heart. She tells herself it must be the money of Mrs. Meinholz that has calcified that muscle of compassion—there should be so much for one and so little for others. It is not just Jan she is thinking of, but the man in the bed beside Jan, and the man beside that man, and across from Jan's ward, the women's ward, and two floors down? The children's ward. One bed after another, one crib after another. Tiny smiling fat faces, cherubs bloated with steroids. So happy to see her, anyone not a doctor with a knife, not a nurse with a needle, with poison. Their hands had reached for her, and they had shouted, *Mamusia! Mamusia! Mamusia!*

Here, a nurse had said, then she handed her an infant. *Make yourself useful. The mother hasn't been back for three weeks. We're not sure that she'll be back in time. He needs to know that he hasn't been forgotten by the rest of us.*

Useful. What is useful?

No matter.

She sat in a hard chair beside a window that overlooked the hospital parking lot.

The boy slept in her arms for two hours.

He opened his eyes, blinked twice, closed them for three more hours.

She did not move. Could not. Would not.

Not even when it grew dark outside.

Not even when most of the doctors and nurses drove away in their cars.

Not even when her arms and legs fell asleep. Not even when her back ached and seized with cramps.

Not even when she knew Jan would be awake, wondering where she was and alone with his waking and his pain.

Only when a nurse, another curt, hurried nurse, with her chart and thermometer and stethoscope reached for him, only then did she move, stand, and in the standing, jarred the boy. *Needlessly,* she thought. *Why? Why wake him, why not let him sleep, wake when he wakes? He's going to die anyway, isn't he?* He opened his eyes. Brown eyes. She wanted to kiss each eye closed again; she wanted to hold his eyes, his gaze in hers, forever.

The nurse tapped her foot: *Rounds—rounds—rounds. Not—the only—dying—child. Another—another—another. Their—loneliness—is—yours.*

The nurse plunked the baby in the crib. His cries, sudden, sharp and hollow, were bereft. She bit her knuckles, tasted blood, and never returned, not even to bring a bag of candy to the older children, not even when she had hours of empty time and nothing but the surety of Jan's death to fill it.

So: she *is* troubled by the uncharacteristic, uncharitable pleasure she takes in stripping Mrs. Meinholz naked each morning, exposing the liver-spotted skin, the breasts wrinkled and deflated, the crotch covered in wiry, gray hair, and all those inexplicable bruises that purple a thigh, a shin, a hip, that bloom on the old by the mere fact that they still move, still breathe, still live.

There is the kowtowing to a few remaining genteel refinements: a shower cap snapped over Mrs. Meinholz's coiffed, silvery blonde hair; a gold watch, winking diamonds; a pearl necklace coiled in the porcelain Limoges saucer by the sink; a towel, warmed in the dryer, hanging over the gleaming silver bar. On a hook, her white bathrobe; on the floor, slippers.

But everything else is done Maria's way—efficiently, without the pointless niceties of discretion. She had tried, those first few days, gently waking the woman with a singsong Good

Morning! Then a small pat on the shoulder. But received only a grunt, a glare, then that terrible, deliberate silence—understandable because it is the silence of humiliation: *I cannot do for myself today what I could do for myself yesterday.* But she has not been hired to assuage humiliations. She has been hired to do and do she must.

So: nightgown and underpants are removed in the bedroom, tossed right into the laundry basket. She prods Mrs. Meinholz into shuffling down the hallway with the walker, fingers under a shoulder blade. Certainly, she is right behind the old woman, vigilant, professionally attentive to any wavering, any unsteadiness, but this is what she thinks watching her inch her naked way down the ten-foot stretch: let her know what it feels to become nothing more than another body, ordinary and poor and waiting to die.

She scrubs Mrs. Meinholz's back in quick strokes, hoses off the soap, then moves on to her feet and its painted toes. Shanghai Red, the color Mrs. Meinholz finally settled on after Maria painted each toe a different shade. As if anyone would ever see the toes again besides the old woman and Maria or run a tongue along the arch, around the ankle, or care if the toes were Splendeur or Organdy.

It is the same reason Maria neglects to think of her own feet as anything but feet. They move her from here to there, keep her attached to here, keep her from leaping off the bridge into there. Feet washed, toenails clipped. She couldn't imagine a man ever imagining her feet again.

"Not so hard," Mrs. Meinholz says, her first words of the morning. And then, "Too soft. Don't they train you properly?"

How do you train anyone properly to tend to a body that is not your own? Or not one you love? The unloved body becomes just that—a body, an accumulation of washable parts, a series of limbs, a canvas of skin, a voice that might start and stop, a staccato fart. You might notice the raised mole changing shape, growing darker, or the splatter of freckles across the shoulder and chest, or the folds of skin at the belly, and speculate: weight gained then lost? a child grown then freed? But you feel nothing towards this body's history, no sentimental pleasure or warmth.

Mrs. Meinholz's eyes are closed against this invasion of privacy, this *manhandling* as she calls it. The old woman had probably hoped for some gentle, soothing presence, some talcum-scented, nursery nurse, someone who, while washing her ass, would not acknowledge this fact. But, Maria argues to herself, she is not my mother and I'm not her daughter and so I don't hesitate to say this: "Pull up on the bar a little more, so I can make sure I've cleaned everything just right. You wouldn't want to smell like caca for your granddaughter, Mrs. Meinholz, would you?"

The granddaughter, Lillian, has been, up to this point, only a beautiful photograph on the wall, a breezy voice at the end the telephone, and one quickly scrawled Get Well card. She is coming to lunch.

Mrs. Meinholz is silent in the strain to raise herself off the stool. Maria holds out her arm. The old woman clutches at it, steadies herself, then says loudly, imperiously, her only means to blot out the mortifications of the bath, "Don't dawdle. I want to be ready when Lillian arrives and there is still my makeup and a table to set, and the food to fetch."

Fetch. What a dog does. Jan had a dog once. Konrad, a fierce brown and white terrier. His before he met her. In jealous complaint, the dog nipped at her heels, barked when she and Jan made love, peed on her shoes. At night though, Konrad curled tight into the bend of her legs, nose to tail, in a kind of détente.

What Konrad fetched: Jan's rank socks, jingling balls, dead mice. What she fetches: the telephone, tissues, nail polish, water, coffee in the morning, tea in the afternoon, one glass of cold white wine at six, pills, pillows, blankets, the mail, the newspaper each morning at seven-thirty from the lobby, a pencil, freshly sharpened, for the crossword, *my* book, *my* bookmark, *my* mirror, *my* purse, *my* checkbook, *my* life, *my* body, bring it back, fetch it for me now, not later.

She understands this tyrannical impulse to order her around. Even Jan, who loved her, was often cruel to her. She could eat kielbasa, pork ribs, trout, donuts; he could only throw up. She could walk to work, even if it was processing stupid government papers, it was something; he could only walk to the bathroom, could only spit bile into the sink or piss in the bucket beside the bed, too tired, too weak, too much in pain to even bother to get up; she could live for many more years; he could only die. She would find him like this when she returned from a few hours at work or from shopping or from a walk in the park, and he would glare at her, the pain inside the anger, the humiliation inside loneliness. *"Get me water. Get me dry sheets. I know you are leaving me. I know you are fucking someone else. Get me water. Leave me alone. Leave me. Let me die. You want me dead anyway."* She brought him water and clean sheets and carried on loving him.

But this is what eats at Maria: the old woman's failings are not so terrible, no real pain, just the expected sputtering out after eighty-three years, and Mrs. Meinholz believes this to be some cosmic injustice. There were the expensive creams and spa treatments, a face-lift, and even, according to the daughter, a personal trainer who had the old woman, at seventy-five, lifting weighted balls and walking to nowhere on a treadmill. While a stroke is not unusual in the old, Mrs. Meinholz had never considered herself to be elderly, enfeebled, needing assistance in living but this is her lot now, like it or not: her left arm hangs limp; her left leg drags behind as if it is weighted with stones; her feet must be shoed in clunky white orthopedic sneakers, an affront to her good taste, to the slingbacks, mules, spectator pumps, and exactly one pair of spotless white canvas Keds that hang in a rack on the closet door.

But Mrs. Meinholz is in her own white-tiled tub, seated on her own plastic white stool, not one pissed on or shit on by an entire, dying cancer ward, being bathed in temperate water with soap that smells of medicine, like healing itself, in the best of conditions by the very same woman who could only offer a perfunctory bedside sponge-down to her own husband.

Jan? At the Wilanów General Clinic, he had to sit on the edge of the metal cot, a thin, yellowed sheet draped over his narrow shoulders because he was always cold, even when the radiators clanged and hissed heat, with his hands cupped over his lap, not for modesty's sake, but in humiliation. He didn't want her to witness the awful indignity of his dying: balls shriveled from chemo; penis a useless, flaccid thing; his body hairless, plucked, vulnerable. But Maria would kneel in front of him, in front of all those other dying men and the brusque, efficient nurses, push his hands aside, and stroke him with the washcloth, cleaning what was so often forgotten by the nurses with their checklists and charts, watches and cigarette breaks, what was so often forgotten by Jan himself. He was a man, a husband, her husband. Hers still. Not dead yet.

Not like this woman—she was not dying of stomach cancer, she was not dying, not noticeably at all. An arm and a leg, that's all that refused to work, and, if Mrs. Meinholz did the exercises, even those could once again be functional. But she had chosen not to try to do for herself: not to eat, not to bathe, not to wipe the shit off her own ass. But she could speak. Not often, of course, to her, but always and on and on to the daughter on the phone.

"Maria has been calling Poland. I have the bill in front of me. Thirteen calls, forty-seven dollars and sixty-nine cents." Then she had thrust the phone at her. "My daughter wishes to speak to you."

Summoned for explanation. How could she have known that telephone companies charge such a fee simply to connect her to Warsaw? She always used a calling card. The agency impressed this upon her. That and to keep her own food on the bottom shelf of the refrigerator since Mrs. Meinholz raised hell over the last aide helping herself to cookies and bread and coffee. She repaid the forty-seven dollars, made it forty-eight, assuming the extra thirty-one cents would mollify Mrs. Meinholz's outrage, but that had gone unnoticed.

This woman was no different from the others she'd taken care of since arriving in New York, failing in the usual ways, lonely, old women who have turned mean in their survival of cancers and strokes and bereavements failed. It was, of course, her own failing, too, that bile—the loneliness of being left too soon—always at the back of the throat, on the tongue and lips.

This word, *bereavement*, so formal. She'd only recently learned the word from a greeting card: *In Your Bereavement* rainbowed across a vase of purple tulips just beginning to unfold. Spring, Christ's passion, rebirth. A foolish card, especially for Kasia. Ludwik hurled himself in front of the morning express train to Krakow a month ago while her sister still snored in bed. It was the only ninety-nine cent bereavement card in the rack. Others were five and six dollars, a waste of money considering *where* Kasia snored (beside Jozef, in his apartment on Debrinksi Street, where she'd lived for the past three years). And there was the postage to Poland and the five hundred American dollars folded inside. *For burial expenses and whatnot*, she'd written in the card.

Whatnot. Another new word, this from Mrs. Meinholz's daughter, Charlotte, who handed her two hundred dollars every week for groceries and *whatnot*.

"Whatnot," she repeated. She was sitting across from Charlotte at the dining room table, a long sheet of glass balanced precariously on strange, twisted steel legs. "What is this 'whatnot'?"

What, not? What nut?

Charlotte continued sorting bills and receipts, circling suspicious expenses. Her black suit jacket was draped over her shoulders and the empty arms hung at her sides like folded wings. Indeed, to Maria, there was something beetle-ish about Charlotte—the glossy black hair sheared precisely in line with her chin, the mouth etched in red, the body cinched inside severe black suits, then always, in an abrupt flash of color, the knotted scarf around the neck. Her body darted and buzzed, everything quick and contained. "This," Charlotte said, underlining *Cosmetics $84.98*. A receipt from the Chanel counter at Saks. "What is this?"

"This is four bottles of nail polish. Your mother did not know what color she wanted. But whatnot? I do not understand."

In the way she'd come to expect, Charlotte raised her thin eyebrows, astonished at such stupidity. "You know."

She shrugged. "I do not think I do know whatnots."

Charlotte rapped her red nails on the glass as if calling her to attention. In addition to being a beetle, Charlotte was a lawyer and often ambiguous, though aggressively so. "You know, whatever personal items Corinne might need."

You know: denture cleaner, denture glue, laxatives, suppositories, Metamucil, adult baby wipes, adult diapers. All whatnots necessary for the upkeep of one's mother's failing body which a daughter will not tend to, will not look at, will only briefly kiss and only upon greeting and only on the forehead.

"Maria, you must be firm with Corinne. My mother has lost her ability to be reasonable. Particularly when it comes to her money. It is your job to help her stay within appropriate limits. One bottle of polish. Not four."

She didn't doubt Charlotte's love for her mother, but it was more managerial than expressive. For instance, the thick red binder sorted with color-coded index tabs presented to Maria when she was hired. She must have looked bewildered because Charlotte smiled and patted her hand.

"I've found it helps to be organized with Corinne. She's very particular. I've tried to include everything about everything here for you in categories that might make sense."

"Could I just ask your mother what she might like?"

Charlotte sighed. "What I meant to say is my mother is particular but fickle. This will provide you with all the options without having to listen to her rattle them off for hours on end."

So: *Burial expenses and whatnots.* No doubt Kasia would give the five hundred dollars to Jozef for his gambling, maybe save a little and buy herself a new winter coat. So be it. Ludwik had slapped her, punched her, kicked her when he got drunk. She lost three teeth trying to redeem him. Jan? He only held on as long as he did because he did not want to leave her, did not want her to be left alone. She had been loved and loved well. Who is she to judge another's bereavement and whatnot?

This tending to the old and ill and ill-tempered is not what Maria had imagined for herself. Her cousin Teresa worked as a seamstress from the basement of her own home, the left side of a bland, concrete, split-family house in Queens, not unlike the prefab housing projects in Wilanów's suburbs. Teresa's husband, too, had died, and she was alone, so wouldn't Maria like to come live with her here, in her house? Couldn't they keep each other company? There were many jobs, if Maria wasn't too picky.

When she said that her cousin was a *seamstress* to Mrs. Meinholz, she could see the old woman thought she meant alterations, hems and buttonholes, straight pins and thimbles.

Something Old World, something appropriately laborious and dull. But Teresa did custom, high-end work for interior decorators—elaborate drapes, swags, and balloon shades in expensive brocades and silks. She had a computer that spit out spreadsheets, a long client list, and an accountant. No prom dresses, no bridesmaids' gowns, no tucks here at the waist or there at the shoulder. Ten and fifteen thousand-dollar jobs for Park Avenue dining rooms and libraries and master suites. Just last week, three thousand dollars worth of jaunty red curtains for a playroom.

What did she imagine for herself here?

In Warsaw, she'd earned a degree in English, but wound up processing building permits. Occasionally she tutored hopeful émigrés, low-level bureaucrats, hapless scientists at her kitchen table or in their dingy offices, pouring over grammar drills, practicing stilted conversations in English about nothing they would ever need to talk about: *This is my pen. Where is the playground? How old is your grandmother?* Nothing exceptional, but adequate. It meant panty hose and her brown, gray, or black skirt; the gold starburst pin on the lapel (a wedding gift from Jan, not gold all-the-way-through, but enough for her all the same) and coral lipstick; a gray briefcase transporting her lunch (ham sandwich, peeled orange, thermos of coffee), a hairbrush, and a silly romance novel. She left the apartment each morning at seven-fifteen and was home by five-thirty. Jan returned from the steel factory at six, showered, then napped on their bed, one leg crossed over the other, arms behind his head. Always, he was startled, apologetic when he woke.

"It's okay," she would tell him. "You work hard. All I do is type into a computer."

They ate dinner together at seven, and perhaps, if the weather was good, strolled in the Wilanów Park, always over the footbridge, pausing for a kiss inside the brick gazebo, stopping on the way back home for a coffee and shared slice of almond cake. They might make love. They might watch the television. Or they might just sleep. Not much of a life, not by Mrs. Meinholz's standards, not even by Teresa or Kasia's standards, but it was their life together and they were content.

When Jan died, what was not much of a life became nothing and she began to think she should die, too. And then Teresa called and said, *Come. I need the company.* Just words, but they were everything.

This new life, though, has not meant living with Teresa but living with the sick and dying. At the beginning, she worked the nightshift for a cleaning company, vacuuming and dusting, emptying garbage cans and sponging coffee spills from counters. Pleasant, monotonous work for eight months until the boss covered her mouth with his hand and unzipped his pants. She kicked him hard and never went back.

So now Maria is here: a seven-room apartment in The Huntington House, a corner building on Central Park West, living in a stranger's home sixteen floors above the city seven nights a week, Sundays off. The apartment is spacious, appointed with beautiful, graceful, esoteric objects acquired in Mrs. Meinholz's previous life of travel. The old woman fills her days by pointing and naming all that surrounds her: apothecary cabinet from China, chandelier from Paris, camel bags from Morocco, kilims from Istanbul, tribal masks from Mali, and china and crystal and sculptures and paintings and vases from just about everywhere else.

Maria's favorite? A four-foot long Victorian terrarium, three tall arches framed in blue and green stained glass, a beveled glass star in the center. Mrs. Meinholz refers to it as her *conservatory*, and each day devotes an inordinate amount of time inspecting the miniature plants for yellowing and rot, for new leaves and buds, the soil for moisture, the windowpanes for humidity. She strokes the fern's ruffled edges, runs a fingertip across the African violet's velvet leaves, trails her knuckles across the moss, primps the dwarf palm's fronds. Sometimes, she wields small clippers, trimming a leaf here, a shoot there, or else plugs in a thimbleful of dirt. Once, she caught the old woman with dirt on her lips, fingers to her mouth. *This is it,* she thought. *Time to call Charlotte. Tell her that her mother eats dirt. The stroke is worse than anyone thought.* But Mrs. Meinholz just lowered her fingers, brushed her lips with the back of her hand, and said, with measured authority, "I was worried about the orchid, but everything tastes balanced."

Who is Maria to say if this eating of the world is imbalanced?

Each day, they sit in one of the apartment's rooms and play fetch. Mrs. Meinholz points to a box or vase or photograph or bowl and Maria carries it to where she sits on the couch or chair or bed. The first time? A blue and white jar perched (too precariously, she thought, though this was a matter for Charlotte to take up with Dominica the cleaning woman who arrives late every Monday and Thursday morning) on the edge of the living room mantle. She'd never looked at it except to note its position, how Dominica dusted it without forethought, slid it along the mantle, then back, had assumed the blue and white splotches were some simpering English flower, the kind of pattern repeated on chintz and wallpaper and china. But when she held the jar in her hands, when she finally looked at it? A fierce, three-clawed dragon: its long, scaled body was a blue flame snaking around the jar, leaping across the tops of the blue waves, clawing at the blue clouds.

"Here," Mrs. Meinholz said, her right hand, the good one, reaching for it. "Arthur and I brought this back from Hong Kong in 1964. Ming Dynasty. Fifteenth century. It is one of my most beloved pieces. A birthday present. His from me." She turned it over, holding it briefly in her left hand, the shaking hand. "This mark, right here, this is how you know it is authentic Ming."

Maria would have told her not to hold the jar in the left hand, would have reached over to help keep the jar steady, but that would only have been met with withering disdain. Let her learn, let her fail.

When the jar slipped, when it shattered on the hardwood floor? The old woman was silent, anger contained, her right hand a hard, white-knuckled fist around the left. Her body, this wreck, betrayed her, ruined the beautiful thing, the damage scattered at her feet.

Maria waited. She could not say, "Let me help you. Let me clean it up for you." She could not say, "I'm so sorry. I know how much it meant to you." She could not say, "I know how painful this is. This loneliness." To offer anything now—it would be unbearable for the old woman. Nothing could soften these small humiliations and losses.

Finally, Mrs. Meinholz said, "The broom and dustpan are in the kitchen closet. There's nothing here to save."

So: Maria swept up the pieces, swept around Mrs. Meinholz's feet, pushed the lame foot to the side, then moved it back, plucked a few shards from the top of Mrs. Meinholz's shoes, then swept them all into the trash bin, save one large triangular piece, a spike of blue, the end of the dragon's tail. She slipped it into her sweater pocket. Worth nothing now, but when it was part of the dragon's whole body? When it completed the vase?

This naming of objects, this storytelling, this strange way of narrating a life through the things that fill its rooms has become their secret ritual. Mrs. Meinholz doesn't speak of it, doesn't announce it, doesn't say, "Now we will go into the living room and commence Show and Tell." She simply shuffles into one of the rooms and calls for Maria to fetch what she desires. Yesterday, from a box beneath the old woman's bed, a silver

Tiffany cigarette case, the husband's, his initials inscribed on the top: AGS. When Maria opened it, seven cigarettes waited inside.

"A pretentious thing," Mrs. Meinholz said, suddenly. "But Arthur always enjoyed the grand gesture. Light one. And don't give me any nonsense about how bad this is for my health." She grimaced with each inhale, smoked the cigarette down with a reverent stoicism, then dropped the cigarette into the glass of water on the bedside table. It hissed out and floated in the gray ash. "You may clean that up now," she said. "And I assume you know not to say anything about this to Charlotte."

Maria smiles. "I only tell Charlotte if you start sneaking the doorman in for wild sex parties."

Mrs. Meinholz doesn't smile, but then she does.

Somehow, Maria already knows not to mention these moments, this recitation of the past, this recounting of a life through the accounting of its objects to Charlotte. It is Charlotte, after all, who often leaves after her visits with a shopping bag secreting something out of the apartment. What is taken is taken on the sly: the ill-fitting mink coat worn on the way out, though not, that she can recall, on the way in; the blender, which was in perfect working order, destined for the repair shop; four rolls of toilet paper and two rolls of paper towels because it was too late to go shopping, though early enough to make a manicure appointment. She knows not to mention this to Mrs. Meinholz who would certainly confront Charlotte, which would be the end of her employment.

Her room, a former guest bedroom, has been stripped of anything of value, the walls painted white, the closet emptied, the bed a single. Maria left most of her own personal items at Teresa's. The bedspread embroidered in red and yellow flowers, her grandmother's once. Her wedding portrait: Jan, so young and serious and ill-at-ease in the navy suit borrowed from his older, taller brother; and she in the wedding dress, its lace itching her throat, the new white shoes pinching her toes. And to avoid any questions, any prying, her wedding ring left inside the candle-well of a purely decorative, crystal candle-stick displayed on the top shelf of Teresa's never-opened china cabinet. For now, all she wants is to be a pair of competent hands.

Mrs. Meinholz waits on her white couch for an hour, studies her watch, asks for lipstick and a fresh powdering of her face, skims a pile of magazines: *Travel & Leisure, La Belle France, Cruise World, Condé Nast Traveler, Horticulture Magazine, The Botanical Review, Fine Gardening.* To travel where, now? To grow what and where besides in miniature under glass?

Each day, Maria offers to help the old woman into the wheelchair and push her down the streets or through Central Park. "It's October," she reminds Mrs. Meinholz, "still warm. I'll put you in a coat, wrap a blanket around your legs, take you to the library or Saks. I'm strong. We can go anywhere." But Mrs. Meinholz will only leave the apartment to be wheeled to the hair salon around the block or doctors' appointments and only if a taxi is waiting at the curb, and will only exit the elevator if the apartment building's lobby is empty and the doorman at her immediate disposal. She refuses to practice with the walker, refuses to be pushed in the wheelchair, and so is left to the occasional shuffle around the apartment, and generally sits all day on her ass on the white couch under a cashmere blanket waiting either to be miraculously healed or, simply and preferably, to die. Consequently, outside of a few trips to the bathroom, fetching water and the pills, cutting poached chicken, steamed carrots, and bananas into small cubes, this is all Maria does, too.

"Perhaps," the old woman suddenly says, "you should call my daughter who might call my granddaughter and check to see if Lillian hasn't forgotten our luncheon."

Maria reaches for the address book on the coffee table.

"No, no need," Mrs. Meinholz says. "Lillian is twenty-four and busy. It is to be expected. It is the right of the young to be forgiven. All we can do is wait."

Maria shrugs. "So wait. But you have the salon at three and they do not wait and they charge you sixty dollars if you come or do not come. And then you will have hair that looks like shit all week." She says this not unkindly.

"Sixty dollars," she'd whispered to Kasia, that first week. "Just to have her hair washed and dried. This is disgusting."

"Why disgusting?" Kasia said, dishes and silverware clanging, cupboards banging open and shut in the background as if to make her point: she'd certainly pay to have such services. "That she spends such money or has the money to spend?"

What she was calculating: what sixty dollars would have bought Jan. Small indulgences to make the dying easier: a private room for the last two days; a private nurse for a week, and morphine, more of it for when he woke, in agony, praying Hail Mary, Mother Mary, not seeing her, not seeing anything, just Mother of God, Take Me. Sixty dollars would have given him peace.

For three weeks Maria wheeled Mrs. Meinholz to the salon around the corner and watched as shampoo girl smiled down at her beatifically, wrapped warm towels around her neck, massaged her scalp, wiped errant soap from her forehead, from the insides of her ears, then wheeled her to blow-dry boy, a blond, muscular, tanned Adonis, who yapped away about his dog and boyfriend, while coiling one-inch sections around an enormous round brush, then spritzing the finished coif in place. All the while, the old woman nodded and snoozed and smiled in stupored bliss.

After the third week, Maria said to Mrs. Meinholz, "I can do this for you. This is a simple matter. My sister is a beautician.

She practiced on me. I watched and learned." A lie. But she had been watching these weeks. Why Mrs. Meinholz agreed to the experiment, she would never know. The shampooing was not difficult, though not as gracefully executed on the stool. And really, she didn't care if soap spilled over into her eyes or ears: the old woman was in the bathtub; she could hose her down at the end.

"Keep your eyes closed, Mrs. Meinholz. Problem solved. Even children know this." She was having trouble lathering up what little was left of the old woman's fine hair; her fingers slipping, sliding across the scalp, washing each other rather than the hair. Already the old woman was shivering, so the rest of Mrs. Meinholz's body would get a cursory scrub down. Odd, seeing her like this, wet from head to toe, hunched on the stool. Like Konrad, the way he used to cower in the corner of the tub, all fierce protest vanishing at the sight of the shower hose. A different dog altogether, with its fur slicked against its body. Not a dog inclined to pee on her shoes, but one that peed on itself in the tub. Not a dog she liked at all.

Somehow, the shower cap had maintained Mrs. Meinholz's dignity. At the salon, she'd seen the bald spots, the liver spots, the wrinkled scalp, but the clothes, the make-up had maintained dignity. But this. This is too close. She sees too much of Mrs. Meinholz. It is why she has left her wedding ring at Teresa's. Mrs. Meinholz would see too much.

One afternoon at the hospital she'd wandered past the crazy ward. The one for old people. She watched them through a window shuffle around an indoor courtyard, bare feet, hospital gowns open at the back, wrinkled asses, some smeared in shit. One woman, nose to a wall, her head covered in white fuzz, her gown in a heap at her feet, her body deflated, utterly still. Unbearable. Is that how she might finally end? Alone? She ran back to Jan.

Mrs. Meinholz raised her hand, halting the procedure, eyes closed against the stinging bubbles. "Do you believe this is merely utilitarian for me? You are paid to tend to my body's waste, to manage its movements, to attend its necessities. There is no pleasure involved. I wouldn't tolerate it otherwise. But at the salon, I buy my body's pleasure much like men buy their whores."

Pointless to continue. Maria rinsed and dried her in the usual efficient, detached way. To offer compassion, to soften her hands and imagine the old woman's body as Jan's? It would be a genuine penance and Mrs. Meinholz would receive this as insincerity, a contemptible, intolerable pity. She would be fired.

So: A warm shawl wrapped around Mrs. Meinholz's still-scraggly-wet head. The salon had an opening. Unusual for a Friday morning. Would Mrs. Meinholz like it? Indeed, yes. Please. Please let her buy her small indulgent pleasure. Bliss for the neglected body.

The granddaughter arrives two hours late and, Maria suspects, hungover. Lillian's smile is tight, deliberate, too wide, her hair gathered in a haphazard ponytail; when she takes off her coat and hands it to her, she can see that the girl has not been home, and, it seems, hasn't eaten in months. Her dress, black with skinny shoulder straps, and her shoes, three-inch silver heels are more appropriate for the night, for fucking, not for lunch at Babcia's. Lillian, surprisingly, leans in to kiss her cheek, and then, after a quick, sly assessment, kisses the other.

Maria can see she is not what Lillian expected, not some dumpy Pole stinking of kielbasa and cabbage. She wasn't so silly to believe Jan when he called her beautiful, but she was attractive in a way: long, proud nose, large, brown eyes, strong cheekbones, straight black hair. It is important to keep up appearances even if you appear to no one, otherwise—and this is a real possibility (it almost happened after Jan died) when you lock yourself inside an empty apartment for three weeks, eating canned tomatoes with your fingers and sipping cold chicken broth straight from the box—you might forget that you appear at all. You might look in the mirror and not see a face, not see a body which might give you the idea to swallow the rest of Jan's pills. So, smudge shadow on eyelids, smear pink on lips, walk, move your body, look up at the trees, the sun, at the world in which you must try to appear.

"Czesc," Lillian says. "Jak sie masz?"

She nods. Someone has been teaching her Polish.

"Lillian, dear, in here." Mrs. Meinholz's greeting is an order.

The old woman is disappointed. Lillian does not eat what she sent Maria out to buy at the expensive little market around the block: chicken salad with pine nuts and raisins, a leek and potato tart, mini chocolate soufflés. What Lillian does have is a glass of white wine, then another, clearly in need of buttressing.

Since Mrs. Meinholz decides not to eat as well, Maria sits pointlessly by her side, listening to their scattered chatter. A movie about some philandering composer that Mrs. Meinholz will not see; an El Greco exhibit at the Met that Mrs. Meinholz will not go to; a poet who is reading his poems that Mrs. Meinholz will not hear.

Lillian turns to Maria. "You might know him. Stanislaw Janek."

Mrs. Meinholz says, "How could Maria know him?"

"He's from Poland, Grandma. Or was. He's been in New York now for ages, ever since he was forced out in the seventies. He's some sort of famous dissident, exiled at some point. He writes in English, not Polish, so maybe you wouldn't know him."

Some sort of famous dissident. Not so famous, just another one of many. But yes, Maria knows him. Knew him. Had, in fact, made love to him many times for an entire year. This was when she was still in the university, before she met Jan, before she loved Jan. Stanislaw, a doctoral student in history. Thin, tired all the time, smoked too many cigarettes, but spoke energetically about what could only be the, if not imminent, then eventual collapse of the regime. She remembers his mouth on her shoulder, his hand between her legs. She remembers his dark apartment, the grim windows, the unforgiving bed pushed into the corner, without sheets, only a rough blanket, as if sleep, as if lovemaking, as if the company of anyone else was unnecessary, unimaginable. She remembers the one chipped white plate, the one fork and spoon, the one mug he kept in the rack by the kitchen sink. She remembers several furtive, hushed phone calls in the middle of the night and how he would slip back into bed afterwards, drumming his fingers on his chest, how he would begin to tell her about whatever trouble he was in, then stop and get back out of bed to piss and smoke and not return until it was morning and she was ready to leave his bed. She remembers coming to his apartment one night and knocking on the door and waiting, hearing him inside, the rustling of papers, the flush of a toilet, knocking again, and shouting, "It's me, Maria," then silence, and then leaving.

But she says nothing of this to Lillian, and Mrs. Meinholz is waiting for her to say, *Of course, no, she does not know this man. He is a poet. What does she know of poets?* Somehow, she cannot imagine him being a poet now, famous in America. This man who once bought her an ugly green scarf, even uglier brown gloves for her birthday. Would he write that poem? But then, would he have imagined her here?

What she does say is, "Yes. I knew him once. A little. We were students at Warsaw University."

"He's my teacher now," Lillian says. "For my poetry work-shop. And my thesis advisor. He's a genius." She reaches for the bottle of wine and pours a third glass.

Maria is mystified. *Workshop.* She knows this word. A garage or shed where you build a rocking horse or fix an engine, stacks of wood, boxes of nails and screws, a power saw and workbench. But a workshop for poetry? Poetry is built in the mind, fixed with words, hammered out in solitude. Lillian goes to school for such a thing? Pays money for this? Is getting a Master's degree in poetry? And Stanislaw the teacher, saying *what?*

Lillian smiles at her grandmother. "Can you believe that Maria knew Stanislaw?"

"You should eat, dear. This food won't keep," Mrs. Mein-holz says.

"What was he like?"

"Maria, coffee." How many grammar drills did she complete for her English degree? Mrs. Meinholz speaks care-lessly because it is her language. But this is what Maria hears because it is not her language: the verb skipped, her name synonymous with the object fetched. So, into the kitchen she goes to…how does the rhyme go? Easy words, simple, uncom-plicated meanings. *Old Mother Hubbard went to her cupboard to fetch the poor dog a bone.* She shouldn't say anything more. This talking angers the old woman, misplaces Lillian's atten-tions. But it's been so long since anyone asked her anything. She pours Mrs. Meinholz's coffee, stirs in cream and a teaspoon of sugar, listens to the silence in the dining room, returns with the coffee.

The old woman raises the cup to her lips in several precise movements. The porcelain chatters against her teeth. Lillian gulps at her wine.

When she speaks, it is to the window and the gray sky beyond it and the life that has long been over. "Stanislaw was a history student. He would sit in a corner table at the café and smoke and scribble in his notebooks." And she on a chair beside him, his foot pressing into hers, though now, it seems, pressing Lillian's. Why else would the girl study their language?

"A student, not a dissident, certainly not a poet, not when I knew him. Though of course, I didn't know him well. So perhaps his scribbles were not historical analyses but poems."

Lillian refills her glass, then claps her hands. "You'll have to come with me to his reading tonight. You can see him again. I'm sure he would be pleased to see you, too."

Mrs. Meinholz clears her throat in protest.

"Grandma," Lillian says, "I'm sure you could manage by yourself for a few hours. Mother could come by if you needed her."

Maria can see the dilemma this has put the old woman in: she cannot admit that she, Maria, is necessary and so cannot say no. But, since she, Maria, is necessary, how can she say yes? A few hours. Only an imbecile couldn't manage this.

Mrs. Meinholz says, "I'm not sure why Maria would want to go to a poetry reading with you, even if she did know the man once."

And truly she didn't want to go, at least, not until Mrs. Meinholz began to speak with such surety of what she might want, of what kind of person she must have been, what kind of life she must have had, which must have been empty and dumb and without consequence.

"If it is okay with your grandmother," she says to Lillian, "then I would very much like to come."

Lillian smiles, finishes her wine, and then leans over the table at her, into her. "Stanislaw will be so pleased. No. Let's surprise him. I won't say anything." She grabs for Maria's hand, pressing it tight between hers. "It must be lonely for you here. I mean not here, with grandmother, but here in general with no one who speaks your language, no one who knows what it was like." The girl's eyes well up, then tears spill over.

What it was like. What sort of fiction has this girl invented for Maria's past? Does she imagine frostbite and bloodied lips? A prison cell and gruel? The frantic dash for freedom? *What it was like:* an ordinary life filled with ordinary love which was for a time extraordinary and now gone. That is what it was like. There is you and then there is what you love and between the two is an ocean which you cannot ever cross. There is no way back. Jan is dead; she is here.

And now this girl holding her hand, crying these big, useless tears. Oh, Kasia would love this show. Kasia would spit at this one, chop the ponytail off at the stump, stomp her manicured piggies in those flimsy silver heels. Crying for the poor Poles, for the poor exiles, for the poor, poor poets condemned to America. Kasia would show her, filch the girl's handbag, run up a string of charges at the nearest Chanel counter: forty-seven bottles of nail polish, sixty-four shades of eye-shadow, seventy-two tubes of lipstick, one-hundred and twelve jars of Youthful Radiance Rejuvenation Skin Cream. Oh, yes, and the free gift. That is what it was like having to live with Soviet make-up.

Why does this girl imagine their solidarity? But then, Lillian is hung-over, verging on drunk again. The offer may be regretted when she is sober.

"Yes," Maria says. "I would like to listen to Stanislaw Janek read his poems and hear what he says about exile."

She doesn't wheel Mrs. Meinholz directly home, has chosen to ignore the skies that have, since they entered the salon an hour earlier, turned a dismal gray, in favor of a stroll through the park.

"I take you on my Sunday walk, Mrs. Meinholz. It is not good to be so much inside without fresh air, without people. Believe me, I know."

"I wish to go home immediately."

But really, what can the old woman do? Wheel herself? Get up and walk, Lazarus-like? Crawl on one hand and one knee for the six blocks? Maria has decided to be firm, to be an aide to health.

"You don't want to become like that poor Brooke Astor." This effectively silences Mrs. Meinholz's protests. No calling out for a policeman. No complaining to Charlotte. She read about that rich old woman in the newspaper. One minute, society balls, luncheons, and trips around the world, the next, Alzheimer's, diapers, and round-the-clock nurses. Her son, a rich CEO, took control of the money, stole everything from her apartment, even her bed, and left her to sleep in her piss on an expensive French sofa, cut off contact with her friends. Finally, someone began to worry and called a lawyer who paid a visit and found her covered in bedsores, malnourished, mostly dead.

She tucks the wool blankets around the woman's legs, over her feet, up under her arms, wraps the blue cashmere shawl in a loose loop around her neck, careful not to disturb the newly-set hair, and pushes off across the street towards the park.

Quiet. Empty. She is glad for this. Mrs. Meinholz relaxes in her chair, her shoulders soften. No danger they will bump into anyone the old woman might know from before, no need to run for cover behind a tree, no need to pretend this wheeling about is a minor setback, a twisted ankle, a sprained knee. So, they have this walk to themselves. But Maria is used to the noise, the busyness of Sunday mornings, misses the meandering couples, the determined joggers, the parents chasing down toddlers, pushing double, triple strollers, the dogs straining at the ends of leashes, and the others, like herself, alone, and—it astonishes her each time—happy for it. She has been walking this stretch of the park for thirteen weeks, enough time to watch the flowers die off, trees lose their leaves. Enough time to feel like she might belong here. Enough time to know she does not belong yet.

"Stop," Mrs. Meinholz said. "Over there." She points to a tall bush growing down the embankment. Its leaves seem, to Maria, predictably yellow. It is October after all.

Maria sidesteps through the muddy grass, reaches to snap off a branch. Surely this is illegal. *Idiot*, Kasia would say, *sent back because you stole dead leaves. You couldn't make it her Rolex?*

"No. Don't pick any. Bring me there. Or as close to there as possible."

Maria pulls a branch down.

"See," Mrs. Meinholz says, "you must pay attention."

Yellow flowers in small, spidery clusters gather at the base of the leaves.

"*Hamamelis virginiana*. Witch-hazel. A lovely surprise. And over there. *Aronia arbutifolia*."

The tree Maria has admired since September when its leaves began to spin to the ground, revealing tight sprays of burnished red berries.

"A chokeberry tree."

"How do you know these names?"

"I haven't always been useless and rich. I studied botany at the University of Wisconsin."

She has heard the name; it is someplace cold, somewhere inside this country, so she nods, continues the walk down the sloping path, across the wooden bridge. No use losing ground now, admitting what she doesn't know. Besides, she is more startled by the fact that Mrs. Meinholz has not always lived in this seven-room apartment on the sixteenth floor, has not always been surrounded by her beautiful paintings and jars and sofas, has not always been part of this city, but has been part of somewhere else, some other life entirely.

Mrs. Meinholz continues, "But then I met Arthur. And that was that. Incidentally, do you know how he came by his money? Valve fittings. A small family company that became a large company under Arthur's direction. A few factories somewhere in the Wisconsin hinterlands. He sold the company to a larger company and we retired to New York. Of course, if you ask Charlotte, she will not admit having anything to do with Wisconsin, though she spent the first twelve years of her life in a place called Sauk City. She was even President of the school's FFA club."

Maria imagines Charlotte in a crisp black suit hemmed precisely to her knee, a white collared shirt buttoned at her neck, knee socks and black patent-leather shoes, her hair in two tight braids, red ribbons tied at the ends, a satchel crammed with her schoolbooks. She imagines her sitting in the back seat of some long sedan, scratching numbers into a notebook, calculating columns and rows of impossible abstract equations, erasing, correcting, perfecting, chewing off the nubbin of eraser, leaving bite marks up and down the pencil.

"What is FFA?" Maria asks. "Future Females of America?"

"Oh dear," Mrs. Meinholz says. "How wonderful. No, certainly not. Future Farmers of America."

At this, they both laugh, but then Mrs. Meinholz is suddenly silent, holds up a hand. Maria stops. What can the old woman see now? Just the path, ordinary bushes, trees, a man slumped on a bench, a woman running at them, her face pinched and sweaty, pushing an enormous tri-wheeled stroller. When the woman huffs past them, feet slapping the ground, Maria hears the baby squalling in protest from inside its strange, zippered cocoon.

"I see how you judge my girls," the old woman finally says. "I may be old and now lame, but I'm not blind and I'm certainly no imbecile. Charlotte may steal from me or take things from me or borrow things from me or whatever it is that she calls whatever it is that she does to make it right with herself. These things are things. What use do I have for a mink coat thirty years out of style? What use can she have for a mink coat five inches too short?"

Mrs. Meinholz twists around in the chair, looks at her, narrows her eyes. What does she see, if she sees her at all? Does she imagine Maria at the American Consulate saying to the Inspector, "My wish is to come to America to take care of your sick and dying because your own children won't?" Does she imagine Maria so lonely, so without anyone at all in Poland that a life taking care of strangers in New York is preferable? She has never asked if a husband, if children have been left behind, though certainly Maria is old enough for there to have been both. Perhaps the question is unnecessary. Mrs. Meinholz must see that Maria is as efficient at loneliness as she is.

"And Lillian?" the old woman says, eyes still on Maria's, as if asking her to see her granddaughter as she does, in forgiveness. "She hasn't been bruised and broken like the rest of us yet. Don't judge her for choosing that man over me. The choice is easy at that age. At any age, really."

Mrs. Meinholz turns away, nods, and Maria pushes on down the path, towards home.

What can the old woman see now?

It is not what is here, not what is before her, but this: the wonderful trick of love, how it overrides what is lost, what has been given up, what has been taken from them.

Arrive early, Lillian said. *It's free so everyone will turn up and we want front row seats.* So. Stanislaw has not saved Lillian a seat. What they have is secret. Or maybe they are not yet fucking and she is trying to arrange for this.

They have been waiting at the front of the line for a half hour, needlessly shielded from the intermittent drizzle by Lillian's umbrella, an enormous satellite with a Georgia O'Keefe imprint, one of those florid, vaginal red flowers. She is careless, bumping people behind them and the one man in front of them with the tines, offering breezy, half-hearted apologies. A shrug followed by a smile: *we are all in this awful rain together so what can you do?* Except everyone else has decided the drizzle is no big deal, will not soak coats, ruin hairdos, or spatter suede pumps. All umbrellas, save Lillian's, are closed. There is no goodwill towards this girl who is chattering loudly about Stanislaw and the cocktail party he has invited her to afterwards, certainly, Maria, you can come though there is a certain sort of unspoken dress code, and a poem of hers (something about a crow eating something dead) that he praised in workshop last week. Maria grasps the edge of the umbrella to steady its aimless bobbing.

"What is Poland like?" Lillian asks.

"Poland?" she shrugs. "I can't say what Poland is like. It is like saying this street is all of America. There are many, many regions. I can say what Warsaw is like, and some of the countryside."

"Okay, then, Warsaw, when you knew Stanislaw. Not Warsaw now when it's just another version of Prague." Lillian says this with the authority. "I made it to Prague when I backpacked through Europe one summer. My last stop before turning back to Paris. It never occurred to me to go to Poland. I thought, factories, sludge, pierogies, ugh. No offense."

And she takes none. The girl wants her to talk about bullet holes and deportations; crumbling Belle Époque townhouses with rusting, baroque ironwork facing off against monolithic Eastern-bloc apartments; atmospheric rain on cobblestone streets and cheap tobacco rolled in newspaper smoked by the pouchful; furtive meetings in dank basements and the romance of desperation, of dissidence, of nascent solidarity; and most importantly, what surely must have been the hard boot of oppression on Stanislaw's back. She wants confirmation that what the poet whispers into her ear while he is taking off her panties is not bullshit.

"Some parts, like the Old Town, are beautiful," she says. "But the beautiful parts were rebuilt after the Germans destroyed them. What is beautiful is only nostalgia. Except for the palaces, Łazienki and Wilanów, everything else is new, like Disney World. Or Las Vegas, how they build copies of the Eiffel Tower or Venice. It is a fake city."

"You were forced to leave, too?"

Maria laughs. "I left two years ago. Poland was free. I was free." The girl is innocent, without history. Or if she is aware of history, it is only her own happy, blameless one. How can she write a poem? How can she feel the weight of language, of what is said and not said?

She, to Jan, *Don't die. Please, don't.*

Jan, to her, *I'm sorry. It is not my intention.*

She to Jan, *I know.*

Jan, to her, *Yes, we do.*

Lillian, irritated, shakes her head. "Not Stanislaw. He had to leave. It was that, or else."

"Or else?"

Lillian's smile is triumphant: her teacher, her lover-to-be is intact. "Prison. Torture. Death."

It is all Maria can do not to laugh again, not because what Lillian says is necessarily an exaggeration, though in Stanislaw's case, likely it is, but because Lillian, knowing nothing of such words, what they mean, how they can carve out your insides, could not imagine that even she, Maria, one of many, not anyone special, not a dissident, not a poet, no one anyone would wait in line to hear, just a wife, and only once, and over already, has been carved out too.

Thankfully, the door opens, Lillian folds the umbrella, and they go inside.

A spotlight shines on the podium. On the small table, three bottles of water, at the far end of the stage, a woman busy arranging books. Many, many books. His. She tries to imagine what he will look like, but can only see a taller, grayer version of Jan—fatter, though, if he's been living in America, eating hamburgers and french fries and tacos all these years. His asceticism couldn't survive this place, not if, as Lillian informed her, he won a Pulitzer Prize, held the New York University Something-or-Other Chair in Humanities, and had already been married and divorced twice. By now, he'd have a cabinet stacked with white china, a king-sized bed stretching from one end of the room to the other, bottles of white wine in the refrigerator, bottles of red in a rack, and money and fame and eager young girls who write poems about cocks and crows.

"That's him," Lillian says, nudging her arm.

Who else would it be?

The girl leans forward, elbows on knees, lips parted, in an artful pose of great expectation: the cat waiting to pounce, to sink its teeth into the back of his neck.

Nothing has changed and everything has changed: his face is merely longer, craggier, his hair still black, though receding on each side of his forehead; he is not fat, just a paunch held in by his suit jacket which he unbuttons with one hand; and his smile, at once composed and offhand, is just the same (though his teeth, no longer crooked, are far too white for a fifty-four year old man who once smoked, and as far as she knew, might still smoke, two packs of unfiltered cigarettes a day).

Lillian's smile is bright, enormous, pleading. Know *me*, smile at *me*, single *me* out of this crowd. His nod back is un-loverlike, wide-ranging, passing across the entire first row. He could be nodding, for instance, at her but he is not. Of this, she is certain. No recognition. But why should there be? She remains, for him, in Warsaw, still twenty-two, her hair in a long, practical braid down her back, a cautious student of English lugging around an armload of textbooks, a disappointed, though not devastated, castoff knocking on his door.

He leans into the podium, grasps it with both hands, anchoring himself to the words that rise and fall and roll out of his mouth, words and words (she can't keep up, can only rest in one word at a time—*silver   tongue   abandoned benediction*), his voice now deep and deliberately, though not unattractively, inflected. The same voice that once said, *Your eyes your mouth I want to fuck you love you be inside you.*

A voice that now says:
a breeze in the lindens
and
airports lonely as freewill
and
the flower's mortal burn

What does this mean? Most of the hour, she is distracted by memories, meandering, perhaps arbitrary, but nevertheless, urgent, insistent memories. A dangerous indulgence as it casts her back into that life she has closed. This return is what happens when she stops moving, doing, tending.

A tiny hand in hers. Kasia's. Fingers pressing her palm. They are standing on the edge of the pool in Korczak Park, lanes crammed with men and women swimming laps, kids splashing, dunking each other. Maria whispers to Kasia: *Close your eyes, you'll be fine, I'll hold on tight.* She won't, of course. She is tired of babysitting her sister; Kasia must learn to swim alone sometime, after all. She lets go. Suddenly, their father is there, hoisting Kasia, who is coughing and crying, from the water, into his arms, into his rough beard, against his hairy chest. "What were you thinking!" he shouts at her. "I was thinking she needs to grow up. I'm tired of having to look out for her," Maria says, hiding her shame, her guilt inside words she will always regret, especially when Kasia shrugs off both Ludwik's bruises and Maria's offer of protection, Jan's protection, their apartment, the couch.

Stanislaw. Driving his battered, red Volgas on a dirt road high in the Swietokrzyskie Mountains. He chews on his lip but says nothing about the strange noises coming from the engine. She worries, too, but is mostly angry at agreeing to his foolish, uncharacteristically sentimental idea: a picnic in the woods. Driving anywhere in that car is always a risk since it sputters and chokes on black smoke at the slightest exertion. The glove compartment, ineptly taped shut, falls open at every deep rut, whacking her knees. "Such an easy thing to fix," she says, "and yet, you don't. Typical." The car stops and they are turning back. Now he is angry, too. "Fuck it," he says, and drinks a bottle of beer in one long swallow, then hands one to her, along with a cheese sandwich wrapped in brown paper. He says nothing for the rest of the sputtering drive back. Not long after this, he decides they are finished and she is left knocking on his door.

Jan pointing to a camera in a shop window. "That one," he says. "For Christmas. I don't need anything else." The cheapest of the most expensive models, what he knows they can afford. His pictures—of skeletal cherry trees in winter, of the Wisla River, of cobblestone streets and graffitied doorways, mostly of her, smiling, not smiling, posed, candid, dressed and undressed, pregnant and then, too soon, not pregnant. All of them left behind with Kasia in four large boxes sealed with packing tape.

And Jan, again. His head in her lap, her hand in his hair, his eyes closed, sleeping. Just, merely, only, thankfully, blessedly sleeping.

• • •

The Exiled Tongue: The Collected Poems, 1978-1999. This is the book she decides to buy. Lillian insists on re-introducing her to Janek. "Plus, you need to have your book signed."

The girl clutches a stack of already-signed books to her chest. She had followed along during the reading, paging to each poem, mouthing the words as he read, jotting notes in a journal.

But why does she, Maria, need his signature? He speaks quickly to each person before her in line, barely looking up, or only looking up to check the time on the enormous clock hanging on the rear wall. He doesn't even try to hide his impatience. And yet, she can also see that he takes great pains with each signature, his hand moving elaborately, dramatically, not economically, not modestly. She doesn't need his signature, doesn't need his inked name inside his book, now her book since she paid the twenty-six dollars. What sort of greeting would he write, anyway? *To Maria, Fellow Pole? To Maria, Who is Here, Too? To Maria, Sorry to Have Left You Like That?*

Suddenly he is waiting, holding his hand out for her book, not yet looking up for the clock, and Lillian is bumping into people again.

"Stan," she says.

He gives her an irritated, closed-lipped smile. It must be the name. Stan. Too intimate? Too American? Too ordinary? The name of an accountant, office clerk, or steelworker? But he does smile, doesn't simply look at the clock, reach for her stack of books, flourish the pen which suggests he has not dismissed the idea of Lillian in his bed altogether.

"This is Maria. Maria…?"

"Palkowska," she supplies. Jan's name. Let him try to place her on his own. Let him remember.

Lillian's hand is in the middle of her back, prompting her forward, to lean in to him, to let him get a good, long look.

"She takes care of my grandmother but she knew you back in Poland, when you were students."

Stanislaw Janek looks up, at her, with what can only be apprehension—eyebrows raised, mouth opening, then closing, trying to summon her face, her name. She notes again those beautiful American teeth. She waits, can feel the line of people behind her growing restless, bodies shifting from one foot to another, their question pressing into her: *Who are you and don't you know you just put the book down in front of him and give him your name and he'll sign his name? Don't waste his time with a guessing game.*

And then he sees her, knows her, the Maria he left how long ago? Thirty-seven, thirty-eight years?

"Maria." Her name in his mouth makes her knees buckle, though not from any romantic longing; it erases time, closes briefly the gap between here and there, now and then: she is not standing here, not the lonely émigré reminding him of their sentimental solidarity (We are Poles together, here in this America!), but lying there, beside him in bed, their legs tangled together.

"It's been a long time, a long, long time. You look well," he says.

"I look old. But then, we are old, aren't we? Or at least older than we were then? But yes, I am well."

He reaches out his hand. Is she to shake it? Kiss it? Press it to her heart?

"I should sign the book?" he asks. His smile, magnanimous, sends a spike of anger through her; it is her right to offer forgiveness, to suggest their ending has been softened by the rosy glow of nostalgia. It *is* her right so she smiles back, opens the book. No need to be petty; they were young and not at all in love and she had Jan, love, happiness.

"And you?" she says. "Have you had a good life? Are you married?"

"Unhappily, twice. I am not meant for love, at least nothing that lasts, as you well know. I am happiest, alas, when I am alone."

If Kasia were here? She'd knock his silly white teeth from his mouth.

But Lillian's uncertain laugh is an accusation: Maria has not been forthcoming. Maria has been oblique. Maria has concealed vital facts. "That's not true," Lillian argues. "I know it isn't."

Stanislaw shrugs. "It is," he says. "You are young and still believe in soul mates and forever after. That is as it should be. But me?" A long, deflated sigh. "I have used up my chances. I'm content in my solitude, though that is not to say I do not enjoy occasional companionship."

Lillian looks at Stanislaw, at Maria, at Stanislaw, at Maria, at his hand now covering Maria's.

A hand whose knuckles are now covered in curls of black hair. A hand that once ranged the whole of her body, brushing her nipples, kneading her thighs, covering her mouth when she cried out so the old woman in the apartment next door wouldn't hear what was going on and complain to the manager. The only other hand belonging to the only other man to make love to her besides Jan. The only man still alive who heard the sounds of her pleasure, her coming, her sleeping, her crying, her being in love, her being—even briefly by this man—loved. And he is here, before her, holding a pen and holding her hand, and she is here, before him, waiting for him to sign his name to his words, waiting, waiting, waiting still.

The apartment is dark and oddly quiet. It is early; the television should be blaring from Mrs. Meinholz's bedroom and the old woman, hearing the door close, the jangle of keys, the rustle of another body, should be calling out to her by now. *Maria! Maria! Water! Toilet! Tea!* Even though she left Mrs.

Meinholz in bed, she had expected to find the living room glaring with light and the old woman sitting on the white couch, rigid, stony-faced, tapping at her watch. Absurd, since Mrs. Meinholz could never get that far on her own. Asleep? Doubtful. She sleeps only four hours, on a good night five and only after midnight.

She finds the old woman on the floor at the foot of her bed, naked, shivering beneath unforgiving light, her wet, urine-soaked nightgown and white underpants folded beside her, one on top of the other as if freshly laundered. Instinctively, the old woman's hands cover her breasts and crotch.

"Why did you try to get out of bed by yourself?" Maria demands, and squats down to pick up the old woman.

Mrs. Meinholz slaps her hands away. "No. No. No." She is seething, humiliated. "I had to go to the bathroom."

"But that is why you have a bedpan. For when you are alone."

"Do you think I want to piss in my bed? Would you piss in yours? Isn't it enough that my leg doesn't work anymore? What other indignities should I suffer? Turds, too? Plop plop plop into the pan where I sleep?"

What can she say?

I know? I had Jan but his stomach turned black and now he is gone? I had a child but my body spit her, him out in awful, bloody clots into the toilet before she, he could become my child and fill my body and fill my arms and fill my heart? That I know the body's cruelties?

No. There is nothing she can say that will give Mrs. Meinholz her body back. If she was Kasia, she might say, "All that is left to you is indignity. Get over it." Even if this is true, she cannot say these words, because isn't this also true? Despite the humiliations, the degradations, the betrayals, the body's progressive, unavoidable failings, aren't there, too, even if infrequent and pathetic and hopeless and hapless and born in anger and not in acquiescence, aren't there, too, the hands folding the nightgown, the underwear? The hands covering the breasts, the crotch, the cock, not merely to hide what is wrinkled and hairless and shriveled, but to announce what is private? Not merely parts, but part of me. Mine.

She hooks her hands beneath the old woman's arms, ignores the slaps, the spit, the spite, lifts her easily, like you would a child. And this body in her hands, this old woman's, is also Jan's. This body, Mrs. Meinholz's, is also hers. This body is, she understands, in its weight and weightlessness, ours, and so she says, "It is time to get up now, Mrs. Meinholz. Get up. Let me help you get up. Please let me help you get up. Let me help you."

Careless

I remember thinking, when we arrived at the top of the hill, that it would have made the perfect photograph, the one to show Mallory and Anna when they were deep in adolescent disdain, believed us ancient and ugly and incapable of pleasure, of ever loving each other, believed that Charlie and I had always been unenlightened despots, naggers, and naysayers. *Homework first. No later than midnight. Not unless I meet him. Don't push it.* What we really meant, each time they left the house and entered the wider world was *Hello. Goodbye. Stay safe. Don't die.*

I'd flip through the album, bypass the pages devoted to their babyhoods, the cheery drool and farting smiles giving way to spaghetti-on-face and days-at-the-petting-zoo, and think: are these sullen strangers really the same astonishing children who wanted nothing more than to wrap their skinny arms around our legs and demand that we pick them up, tuck them in bed, and never leave?

Mallory would point to each of her photos and ask, "What was I like then? And then? Was I happy then? Were you and Dad happy then? I loved this rainbow dress. I bet you threw it away. You never saved anything of mine."

She'd pout, but I'd keep turning the pages.

And Anna? She'd realize again and again that she was never just one, but always the younger half of two. "You always lined us up in the same dumb pose," she'd say. "I'm always off center. And my hair is always in that stupid Princess Leia. What's up with that?" She'd roll her eyes at Mallory.

Then I'd say: "I want to show you something, a perfect day. Don't you see?" I'd lie, "We were young, too, and easy in our happiness."

Late September, the four of us—Charlie, his brother Peter, Peter's wife Naomi, and me—sprawled across a cotton quilt beneath a massive burr oak and its extravagant crown of red leaves, our teeth and tongues stained purple, plastic goblets in hands, our talk drowsy and insubstantial, coasting across the edge of the day. An empty wine bottle cast off in the grass, a second that Charlie poured out evenly between us. We'd hauled beach chairs and a tray table, along with a goat cheese tart, arugula salad, blueberry cobbler, peanut butter and jelly sandwiches, Mallory's new bicycle, and industrial-strength bug spray, dragging it all across the marshy field and up beyond the top of the hill where it was dry, away from the muck of a lake, its incessant mosquitoes, and the idiot on his dirt bike spraying mud, zigzagging across the meadow. For weeks, it had been raining, the sky an oppressive lid above the trees in town, everything a dull, vacant gray. This was our first reprieve.

The girls rooted around in the long grass, digging up slugs, stirring earth. I could see their blond hair glinting in the sun and called to them every few minutes just to make sure Anna hadn't swallowed a rock or Mallory wasn't feeding one to her. "Anna's okay, Mallory? You're the big sister, the one in charge over there. We're counting on you."

Mallory shouted back that she was okay, they were okay, though Anna was stink-a-roni, and somebody'd better come change her diaper right away before she was in deep doo-doo.

"In a minute," I said. "I'll be there in a minute," but made no move to get up. My head was in Charlie's lap, the sun on my face, and his fingertips tapped code against my forehead. *We'll be okay. Stop. We'll make it work. Stop. It's only temporary. Stop. Right?*

Naomi rapped her wineglass with her fork. "Kiss," she demanded, "kiss. Picnics require romance. Lechery at least."

Beneath me, Charlie's thighs clenched, his blue eyes fixed on mine; he was no longer able to take such a humdrum liberty for granted. I pursed my lips and he leaned over, his brown hair brushing my chin. A quick, unconvincing upside-down kiss. Then I sat up, shifted away from him, and Charlie turned, feigning interest in a couple of turkey vultures circling above the woods, their broad, dark wings spread out against the sky.

"Something's dead in there," he said.

We had not said anything to anyone about our imminent separation. It was still a private fact, something we whispered about after dinner, after the girls were sleeping and the house quiet. It is not divorce, we said, not the end. Just a way to gain perspective: better apart or together? No one banished to the pullout couch and its sharp coils that pricked through the mattress, no clothes tossed out the bedroom window and into the gutter, no lawyers consulted. We still slept in the same bed, rolled towards each other, reached for each other, made love even, though it was a lonely kind of love, tentative and regretful, already implying a bed empty of the other, empty of arms and legs and dreams. But on this day, we were what we would call happy, nothing final, and the world did not yet know. It could still never happen.

Naomi sighed. "Not bad for Pavlovian response. It's the first one I've seen all weekend." She was bundled in one of my thick Peruvian sweaters, a geometry of teal, red, and black that hung almost to her knees and her red hair fastened with a silver and coral clip. She had promised the clip to Mallory—all weekend Mallory had been fingering the clip whenever it wasn't in Naomi's hair, tracing the silver swirls, then circling around and over the tangerine stone.

"It's too much," I said. "She has to learn she can't get everything she wants."

Naomi raised her eyebrows. "Debra, let up a bit. She gets whatever she wants from me. Right, kiddo?"

Mallory was delighted. Her eyes, hungry and desperate, slid to the clip in Naomi's hand. "I'll be careful. I'll never lose it. Never ever never."

I shrugged, too tired to do battle with either of them. Already there had been Anna's tantrum: the bathwater was too cold and she had to come out. She'd kicked and screamed for what seemed hours, sending water across the floor, soaking my shirt and jeans. I slumped over the tub's edge and cried great big stupid crocodile tears. Silently though, not wanting anyone, especially Anna to know, because after all, she was just being two, doing what she was meant to do when faced with hands that would wrench her from the tub, with bedtime and darkness and loneliness waiting afterwards, with the big bad will of Momma that was stronger than hers. I was just overwrought from it all.

So, Naomi gathered Mallory's hair in her hands, then shut the clip closed, like a talisman.

Peter sat at the edge of the blanket, his back to us, knees drawn to his chest, watching the red-winged blackbirds dart in and out of the cattails at the lake's edge. The birds screeched at each other, at anything that threatened home turf, launched themselves into a fit, skimming the tops of the stalks, nearly grazing their bellies, then settled on top of the brown seed heads. The stalks bowed under their weight. "Incredible," he said, over and over. "They never fall."

Naomi nibbled at her tart and blurted, "I've never seen so many fat people in one place. It's depressing, really." She lowered her voice in apology. "How do you stand it?" A long slug of wine, then her hand, for reassurance, felt for her hipbone that jutted above the waistband of her jeans.

I shrugged. "Winter isn't kind. Months and mountains of snow. What else is there to do but eat?" Last winter, our third one here, I'd gained ten pounds, which I'd since lost along with ten more. Who can eat when you're marking little red x's on a calendar: this will be the weekend you fly to New York to see the girls; this will be the one I drive them to you.

"You made a baby," Naomi said. "Anna's something. Something we haven't been able to do."

Peter looked over his shoulder and said, "You have to have sex for that."

Naomi needled him with her foot. "We'd actually have to be awake in bed for *that*. All we do these days is collapse into comaville."

Which wasn't true. They'd been making a ruckus every night, every morning, every nap they took since arriving. I'd seen the look of charged relief they gave each other in the middle of our chaos, the girls howling and whining and squabbling, Charlie and I shifting responsibility—*your turn to change what needs changing, to fetch what needs fetching, to sing what needs singing.* We reminded them that they could still be gloriously selfish, and retreat, mid-afternoon, to bed and nakedness and pleasure.

Anna, I thought, and listened for the girls. Anna's voice first, a high chatter. To eat or not to eat the grass? Then Mallory's, with the wisdom of six: "Yucky, yuck. Not in your mouth."

Below us, the dirt bike buzzed out of the stand of pines and aimed for the lake, scaring up the blackbirds. "Asshole," Charlie muttered. "He thinks no one else is out here?" The motorcycle disappeared again back into the woods.

"Inertia is terrifying," I said. "Everybody I know here is on Paxil or owns a lightbox or their skin is suntan-booth-orange." In winter, snow banks, blackened and yellowed with dirt and dog piss, hulked along the roads. Hardly anyone shoveled sidewalks or scattered salt on the ice because no one really walked anywhere. We waited it out inside, curtains drawn, extra blankets hanging from the rods, the drop ceilings pressing down, the awful dark paneling on the walls pressing in. Even in spring, when the pale, distant sun finally broke through, the only things illuminated were the empty storefronts, the only places to go to were the Church of the Living Waters of the Precious Saving Blood of Jesus! and Alcoholics (not so) Anonymous. How could anyone be happy in our tiny, cramped house? A rental, still, even after Charlie's tenure was assured because who would want to buy here, invest here except those with money and time to burn?

Our first year, I'd felt emboldened, giving the city the slip, taking on the country life and its test of seasons. We'd have our own house, Mallory her own room instead of the cheap screen accordioned across ours, dividing her toddler bed from our queen. And a garden in our backyard with tomatoes and squash twining stakes, and rosemary and basil rooted in the ground instead of on the fire escape in milk cartons. Newly pregnant with Anna, I'd welcomed the insularity of such domesticity.

The second year? Meant to build reserve and determination, scour clean any naïve expectation of rural bliss. Was my will greater than our failure to thrive? The summer was too rainy and cold for much of anything to grow except milkweed and dandelion and mold. And then last winter, there had been the almost-suicide of Charlie's student, his best, and he fell away into work and scotch and silence.

Naomi shook her head back and forth. "I could never live anywhere but California. That guy on that stupid bike would be arrested in a heartbeat. Can't the college open a satellite campus somewhere near anywhere instead of nowhere? We'd visit more often, you know."

"You can't teach Tolstoy without winter and melancholy and loneliness," Charlie said.

"Don't you miss the city?" Naomi asked. "What do you do?"

"Drink," Charlie said, "and fuck. Flee whenever possible."

Though I laughed too, I made a face and said, "That's not true. You also have your writing and students who love you and your classes. You should read his evaluations," I said, shaking my head. "*Professor Manning really cares about us on a personal level. He even lets us call him at home when we need to talk about our work. Professor Manning is demanding but he always makes time for us even when his office hours are over.*"

Peter smiled in admonishment. "You never could say no to a co-ed in need. Especially if she bats her eyes and pleads ignorance." His voice became syrup. "Please Professor Manning, are my sex scenes realistic? You know, you actually can do it in handstand position. Besides, you always tell us to write what we know."

I laughed; Charlie didn't because it was true. His students spilled their most secret lives onto the page and called it fiction.

"It's not like that," he said finally, running his finger around the edge of the glass. "You have to listen. They've just handed you twenty pages of what is, of course, absolutely 'not autobiography.' It only *resembles* their lives in its details, and they want you to tell them the story is great, the characters complicated and interesting and daring and what else? Oh, yes, original. I don't. I tell them what's shit, what's tired melodrama, what's empty, and instead of hating me, they want more. It's all very masochistic."

"And seductive," Naomi said. "I don't know how many crushes I had on my professors, especially the ones who gave me a hard time. And sitting there in their cramped offices, piles of books spilling down the shelves, my knees trembling, hoping for some sign that they could see into me, not through me. So, Charlie's out making girls tremble. What do you do, Debra?"

Charlie looked at me, his gaze steady and even, willing me to keep it light.

I smoothed a ruff of grass back and forth and said, "I run on the treadmill and wait for Charlie to come home. And of course, Mallory and Anna are happy enough here. They have all the room in the world."

I looked across the field at the girls still torturing slugs. Since our move to the sticks, Mallory had taken up bugs, chucking her headless Barbies into Anna's room. Beetles and moths thrummed inside jars on her dresser. On the back porch, there was a bucket of worms that, to her great distress, was quickly picked clean by Blue Jays. She wore a magnifying glass around her neck on a string, and in her pocket kept a spiral notepad on which she jotted odd hieroglyphics and diagrams. When Charlie and I argued, she tore out pieces of notepaper and handed them to us, or slipped them under our closed bedroom door: *Stop yelling*, she wrote. *Be nice.*

I said, "So they need me and I need them, and the students need Charlie and I don't know what Charlie needs, but whatever it is, it keeps us from sticking our heads in the oven. Isn't that what saves us? Someone needing you, and you needing them and following through?"

Charlie always had a line of students at his door wanting him to give more, read more, listen more. What surprised me was how much I'd come to resent them, especially the ones who called incessantly and at inappropriate times: I'd be on the toilet or Charlie would, or he'd be standing naked in our bedroom, just out of the shower, and he'd pick up the phone and chat about structure and character development, his penis just hanging there. I resented him, too, the way he'd be up into the late hours of the night reading their stories, scritching his pencil across the pages, demanding substitute words, alternate endings, thinking about them and their phrases and what they meant or didn't mean, instead of us, instead of me.

Thinking instead about Elizabeth, the girl who almost died. All semester she had dropped her stories in our mailbox in the middle of the night, on weekend nights, the pages scrawled with hasty, penciled revisions. Or she'd show up on our porch after class, after a fight with her boyfriend or parents, after a bad, bleak night, her eyes blank and hollow, her pale hair hanging in her face.

Initially I'd been sympathetic, if for no other reason than to have her recover, to get well, take her lithium or whatever drug she was on that would reverse the decline. So, I'd brew tea and bring it to them on a tray along with lemon bars or oatmeal cookies, feeling like the kind, gentle version of my regular exasperated self. Elizabeth talked herself out, while Charlie sat across from her, bent forward, hands on knees and head in hands. It was what he could do, what he must do, what anyone with daughters would do, wasn't it? At least for a little while, I agreed, until it became too much, until he became the only place for her to go.

And when she seemed better, or at least resigned to go on, Charlie would squeeze her shoulders, or sometimes give a hug, though I'd warned him about getting too close, since he didn't want anyone, the school, surely, or Elizabeth, certainly, misconstruing his intentions.

A few times she stayed for dinner at my urging, when I could see she was not yet so resigned, when I couldn't see turning her out to her narrow dorm room, its cinder-block walls, and ramen noodles cooked in a hotpot. I fed her on our happiness. Mallory tugged at Elizabeth's hand and pulled her upstairs to her bedroom and the shoeboxes of cicadas and beetles and bits of moth wings, everything that had died off in her jars that fall. Elizabeth was patient and interested, asking about their names, what she had fed them, how long she'd been able to keep them alive. And when Anna wailed in her highchair, Elizabeth took out the crayons and drew pictures of suns and moons, cats and dogs, flowers and smiley faces. I stirred the spaghetti sauce and didn't mind setting the extra place at the table.

After months of this, though, nothing was better, and then one night after we'd been out and Elizabeth babysitting, I found her lying on our bed in the dark, head on Charlie's pillow, the rest of her under the bedspread, eyes closed. She was startled when I woke her but not embarrassed, not apologetic. She slid from the bed, felt for her shoes on the floor. "I didn't think you'd mind."

"I don't understand why you're in here," I said, my goodwill at its end. "This is our bedroom. You're in our bed." What else had she been in? Charlie's study and the file cabinet and its one file crammed with our early, silly love letters? My closet and its pathetic stack of Rescue-My-Marriage books I'd secreted beneath sweaters? Did she watch our shadows cross each other against the pulled shades, and when the lights went out, mistake our sleep for rest?

• • •

"She's desperate for company," Charlie said, his voice sad and final, stating what was also the matter with him. "I can't just cast her off. Not after I've let her in?" As if he'd caught her with one of those monstrous treble hooks from his tackle box, the three barbed prongs buried deep in her skull. As if, after the painful, bloody unhooking, she'd be thrown back into the swampy muck of her life, forced to bear it alone.

He was scrubbing dishes, staring out the window into the back yard. At what? The picnic table buried under snow, the darkening sky, the finger of God damning him to whatever circle of hell Professors-who-fuck-with-their-students go to when they get careless, cause damage?

He said, "You can't pretend you're not part of it."

Anna squatted on the floor, scribbling across the pebbly linoleum with a fat red crayon. She looked up; her smile was open and generous, demanding only that we pay attention, love her extravagantly. Mallory was slumped against the doorway, twisting a lock of hair tight around a finger, her face troubled, waiting for me to explain why Elizabeth couldn't stay for dinner anymore, why she couldn't babysit anymore. Her Elizabeth recited bug limericks on demand (*I once met a spider named Lily, her skinny eight legs were so silly... There was a big beetle named Bert, who secretly crawled down my shirt*); she participated in elaborate, entomological fantasies (all fours on the ground, they scoured the dank corners of the basement or turned over rocks and rotting logs in the backyard); she did not crawl into her parents' bed or hold her father against her longer than necessary in those magnanimous hugs or late night calls, breathing quietly into the phone.

I said, "Sometimes people are sad because they can't remember how to be happy. Or they don't have enough people who love them. Or they love people too much," I said.

Mallory shook her head and frowned. "No," she said. "That's a lie. You can't love anyone too much." Her look was fierce and unforgiving, moving back and forth from Charlie to me and it said: *you and you, you and you, you two.*

But someone else needed to be responsible and I insisted Charlie call the Dean of Students who was, after all, trained to deal with this. Whatever he said to Elizabeth kept her away. On a frigid March night, a few weeks later, campus security found her in a ravine behind the dorm, barefoot and in flannel pajamas, an empty bottle of pills in her pocket, head resting on her rolled up jacket. Charlie went to the hospital to explain how it had become necessary for him to inform the school, that it was required that he let those that could help her know what was going on. She picked up the plastic water pitcher beside her bed and threw it at him. Then she was gone, back home, back to her family and out of ours.

My glass was empty. I'd finished the last quickly, too quickly, but then, that's what this week was about: the two cases of wine and the fresh-frozen, free-range duck and wild Coho salmon Peter and Naomi shipped ahead from California; the goat cheese logs and the triple crème Boursault in plastic containers beside the bubble-wrapped jars of chutneys and olive oils and the Meyer lemons picked from their lemon tree inside their suitcase.

"Gifts from the Promised Land," Peter had explained as he unpacked it all onto our kitchen table.

"I'm surprised you got all this through security," Charlie said, sniffing at one of the rounds of cheese. "This could knock out an army."

We'd been up three nights in a row until well past two, drinking and eating too much, smoking the pot Charlie had stashed in the back of the freezer and forgotten about until now, pretending we weren't stuck here in the abysmal town, weren't roused by soggy diapers at six-thirty in the morning, weren't trying to make ends meet on one assistant professor's salary, weren't inching towards us being over, but were lolling around Tuscany or Provence, free to do anything, be anything, to choose our lives once more.

This was what the separation was about: would we choose each other again?

Last night, Charlie and I said goodnight to Naomi and Peter, our arms around each other for real and not for effect, and stumbled upstairs together. We were always better when other people were around, and nicer to each other, too, bumping hips in the kitchen, begging pardon, and excusing it. Our guests expected us to be happy, and so we were. Charlie followed me into Anna's room and we stood beside her crib watching her sleep. She'd scuttled into the corner of the crib, her body wedged against the bars, hands bunched beneath her. She was, I realized, as close as she could possibly be to the door, the way back out to us.

"Are we making a mistake?" he asked.

"Of course," I said. "But what else can we do? Neither of us, really, is happy anymore. You know that. Even Mallory knows that."

He drew the covers up around Anna, kissed his fingertips, and touched her forehead. "You'll come back," he said. "You won't stay away forever."

What did I know then? Nothing. I had never known my life, my adult life, without Charlie, did not know if it would be easy to stop knowing someone. We had married right out of college, and I'd followed him to Chicago for his degree, then New York City for a fellowship, and then this town, this place of one mediocre college, one Chinese restaurant, one Burger King, and one hair/tanning salon, L.A. Glowmation, a geographical fantasy of a warmer, sunnier clime. There was no one for me to be here except a wife, the girls' mother, and I needed more, though what that was I could not say. Somehow I believed that staying with my mother in her tiny walk-up apartment in Manhattan would help. It was a life that would be full of everything but Charlie, and I wanted to find out how soon, or even if, I'd feel the emptiness of that.

Stay away forever? "No," I assured him. "We'll be back in a few weeks." We shut Anna's door behind us, carefully, slowly. If she woke up and saw us leave, she'd be inconsolable.

I'd just spooned out heaping plates of the blueberry cobbler when we heard the whining buzz of an engine coming closer, growing louder, going too fast. We all looked down the hill: the dirt bike tearing up the hill, oblivious to us all. Mallory and Anna were still crawling around in the grass, thirty, or forty yards away. Charlie bolted off the blanket and took off, a wine bottle brandished over his head like a mace. Peter scrambled up, too, shouting and waving his arms overhead. Naomi screamed, "Stop him. Stop him. Stop him." I was on my knees, pinned in place, hand to mouth, helpless: there was no way any of us could run the distance, could reach the girls before the motorcycle reached them. Not even their father.

And the girls? They were no more than shadows in the hill and grass with their backs to us and to the dirt bike gunning for them.

He shot over the hill in a roar of engine, and seeing the girls at the last second, veered away over the rise. He wasn't even close, though he wasn't far enough. Inexplicably he stopped and cut the engine, resting one black-booted foot on the ground.

Did I imagine the immediate and endless silence of that moment? That everything, even the grass and the slugs and the blackbirds and the sun and the shadows, held its breath as the strange, mud-spattered helmet turned right towards the four of us, then left, then right, and left again? What he saw, what was finally coming into view was hidden from us behind the dark visor.

"You fucking fuck," Charlie shouted, splintering us all apart. The bottle was still raised menacingly in the air.

The helmet came off. He couldn't have been more than fourteen or fifteen, his cheeks livid with pimples, a shock of red hair curled against his forehead.

Charlie and Peter closed in.

"I'm sorry," the boy said. "I didn't know."

Charlie lowered the bottle, but I could see he was ready to sock the kid, knock him right off the bike to the ground. "Do you know what you almost did? Goddammit. Do you see?" He moved in close. Did I imagine his finger poking him hard in the chest? The boy leaning away, his eyes wide, afraid? That I hoped a bruise would bloom across his heart?

The girls were standing up now: Mallory holding Anna tight against her side, Anna whimpering.

"Momma!" Mallory called. "What's happening?"

"Stay there," I shouted back. "Don't you dare move." I was afraid for them even to cross in front of the dirt bike, as if, thwarted in the first go around, it would jump out from under him and cut them down. This was what I had seen, after all, so finally and completely, as I knelt on the blanket in the middle of the clutter of bottles and plates, in the middle of the sun and leaves: the dirt bike vaulting over the hill and falling with its unforgiving weight upon them.

I had to let them back in slowly because it could have all ended so differently. Look, I said, to myself, to put my heart back in my chest: Anna's hand is in Mallory's, Mallory's hand over Anna's. Their bodies, one small, the other smaller, are standing straight and perfect, not damaged, not smashed, not dead.

The kid looked away from the girls. "I'm sorry," he said again. "I didn't see you." He had a stupid idiotic kid face, incapable of imagining the worst, the end.

Charlie glared, not buying it. "You didn't see us sitting here under the tree on the top of the hill? Bullshit."

"Sir, I'm sorry. I mean, I saw you, which is why I went this way. I just didn't see them." He couldn't look toward the girls this time, or at Charlie and Peter and the bottle still between them. He turned to me.

"Get out of here," Charlie said, his voice level and mean, and swung the bottle in the direction of the woods. The kid nodded, kick-started the bike, lowered the helmet, and drove off. We listened to the engine's distant whine and then nothing except for the rustle of leaves and the girls' excited chatter and my breath moving back in and out of my body.

"Fuck," Peter said. His hands were on top of his head, like a man under arrest, and then he fell to his knees. "What the hell just happened?"

A near miss. Or, if I am being objective, am not being Mallory and Anna's mother, a far miss. Ten yards? Fifteen? Close enough that I'd never let it go. How careless a bit of easy happiness can make you. But it was nothing the girls would ever remember. Or if they did, then it would be a day marked by the slug and mud pie smoothed to a finish across the sunflower plate. Or the long view of their parents murmuring under the tree, laughing again. Or the tall tree itself, its crooked limbs and red leaves flaring in the sky. Or the kid's padded jacket, the orange flames burning down his sleeves and across his chest. A man on fire.

Another near miss: When the college called about Elizabeth at six a.m., an alarmingly early hour for administrators, Charlie had answered. I was in the shower, dragging the razor up my legs, no shave gel or soap, just water, running out of time. Anna woke at six-thirty with a ravenous caterwaul from her crib, Mallory reluctantly at seven. I had fifteen minutes to fix myself for the day before I raced between the upstairs and downstairs, prodding Mallory along, trying not to get irritated by her ten minutes of indecision over flower underpants or polka dots, then shoveling oatmeal into Anna, wiping up the deliberate glops she flung to the floor, trying to keep her in the high chair when all she wanted to do was climb out.

Charlie drew back the shower curtain, his face long, devastated. "Elizabeth is in the hospital," he said.

Though the razor jumped and sliced into my shin, I was not surprised. She had called several nights before, too late for anyone to call except with bad news, her voice thin and plaintive, asking for Charlie.

I dropped the phone in the middle of the bed and walked into the narrow hallway. At its end, Charlie's study, the door closed, a bar of light at the bottom. He was still marking papers or writing or stalling, maybe jerking off to women spread eagle across his computer screen. Who really knew those days what he did for all those hours in there? But he wasn't in bed with me.

"Why won't he talk to me anymore?" she asked, frantic when I had informed her he couldn't come to the phone. "What did you say to him?"

"Look," I said evenly, "he hardly talks to me anymore, so frankly I don't care why he doesn't talk to you. Did you ever think you just wear people out? You're not Charlie's daughter, not his *anything*."

I told no one about the call, about her threat. I simply hung up the phone, slipped back under the covers, and hoped for the best: that the damage would be minimal and contained.

When Charlie stood at the edge of the tub, distraught over that girl, panicked even, his hand grasping for the edge of the curtain, for the wall, for my hand, anything to keep steady, as if nothing else mattered but how he failed her, I blandly watched the blood trickle down my leg, swirl down the drain, and shrugged. "Maybe it's for the best," I said. "She'll get the help she needs now."

"When did you get like this?" he said, stepping back in disgust.

"Like what?" I drew the razor in slow, purposeful strokes over my knee.

But he didn't answer and then he was gone, back to the phone and the administrators, back to his office, his work, his students, and his brooding flagellation.

I rinsed the razor, set it on the edge of the tub, and got down on all fours, my forehead butting the porcelain bottom. I stared down the dark drain as if into the bowels of our house, and retched.

We didn't leave our picnic. Not right away. Mallory, sat cross-legged beside Naomi, happily munching her peanut butter and jelly sandwich, complaining that I'd used grape jelly instead of strawberry. She peeled off the crusts and mashed them into her pockets, saving them for the blackbirds. Her face was streaked with mud, which was also caked beneath her fingernails. Anna toddled in figure eights between us, stepping on fingers, knocking over the empty wine bottles, which I'd righted on the blanket. Mallory had woven a crown of green moss into her hair. In her palm, a squashed slug. My little swamp fairies.

There was still sunset. And if we ignored the tire ruts and churned up grass, we could salvage the day. It hadn't all been ruined.

Charlie uncorked the last bottle of wine, his fingers jittering, and poured it all out at once. "I almost hurled this at him. Just to make him stop. I was aiming for his head."

Naomi twirled a leaf under Mallory's chin. Mallory giggled. "The police would understand," she said thoughtfully. "Anyone would. Protecting your young. Besides, I'd imagine it's illegal to ride that here."

Charlie shrugged. "Who can tell? Schools close for the opening day of deer season. Buck day, they call it. It's all about spilling blood and guts around here." He was scanning the woods, still holding the bottle, though it was empty now, as if intent on catching sight of the dirt bike or its back tire or the smooth skulled helmet, hoping he could throw that far. But the trees were still, the woods silent.

"I imagine alcohol's illegal," I said, then reached for Anna. She squirmed, kicked at my hands, twisting away. Her pants were damp, her diaper heavy with poop and pee. When had I last changed her? Hours ago? Too long.

"You didn't bring the wipes?" I said. Did I? They weren't in any of the bags or lost under the picnic blanket. Maybe in the car?

Charlie said, "You packed up the girls like you always do." He drained his glass and threw it down the hill. "Now I won't have to remember to forget that, too."

Naomi tried not to look at me as she handed over a wad of napkins. I lifted Anna's legs, wiped her bottom clean as best I could, and kissed her belly. "Smelly belly," I said. She didn't laugh, just cried harder as I tugged her pants back up.

"No," she said. "No, no." She sprang up and smacked me on the cheek, then darted over to the tree and Charlie, clutching at his legs.

I knew I deserved it. *Wake up. Pay attention. Be Momma.*

"Of course," Peter said out of the blue, as if continuing some forgotten conversation, "what we were doing was steering him right into the girls. Like those guys with the flags on runways. He was veering right to avoid us." He stared out over the field at the space the girls had filled.

Charlie was taking this in slowly, backtracking: the wine bottle over his head, the kid, terrified, changing course, careening over the rise toward Mallory and Anna instead of us. He kicked at the tree, jamming his foot into the bark, chipping it off.

"Please," I said. "Don't talk about it anymore. It was just some dumb redneck kid who probably feels terrible now."

Charlie laughed and sat back down on the blanket, at the farthest edge from me. "They think they can do what they want with their guns and their bikes. Tear up a park? Run over a few kids? *Hey, they were in my way.*"

Naomi laughed. "Force feed him tofu. That would be good punishment, don't you think? With one of those long funnels they use for geese. Turn his liver into soybean foie gras."

"Then cut out his heart," Charlie said.

"Stop," I said again. "Mallory, honey, don't listen to Daddy. He's being silly."

Her eyes were wide, her hands folded tight in her lap. Did she imagine the worst? Her father hunched over the kid, a bloody heart thumping in his hand?

"Impossible anyway, Mallory," Charlie said. "People like him don't have hearts."

Which is what he had said to me, too, when I first said I was going to New York with the girls. Just to get some distance, some breathing space. "You don't have a heart, do you?" he said. "Because if you did, you couldn't do this."

We were in the kitchen and it was late, too late for the conversation since we'd already had a bottle of wine and Charlie had a set of stories to read.

"I'm tired of this," I said, tipping my glass over. What was left spilled onto the table. Behind us on the counter, Anna's monitor hummed. Every now and then, she'd snuffle or turn over and then it would crackle to life.

"What is *this*, Debra?"

"This place."

"And the girls? How am I supposed to live here without them?"

"You get home after they're asleep as it is, and on the weekends, you hide away in your study writing. Think of this as an experiment. A few weeks to live your life as you want without guilt, without anyone expecting you to do anything else."

"I just didn't think we were at *this* place yet," he said.

Anna coughed, the monitor squawked, and then she wailed.

"Don't," Charlie said as I began to get up. "Let me go."

I said *this place*, but what I meant was: *you*. And what I meant was: *me*. It was true that I felt hard, less generous, less forgiving here. When Elizabeth called that night, and I said what I said, with my heart in my fist, what I meant was: *Charlie already has his daughters and I'm tired, too, and alone, too.* I told no one about the phone call, just as I told no one how one night, I got out of bed and tiptoed outside. My feet were bare and I was only wearing a thin cotton nightgown but I stretched across the ice-hard snow in a corner of our yard, away from light, and closed my eyes and wept for what I had done and failed to do. When the cold became too much, my body seizing and aching and burning with it? I didn't move but waited until I was filled with her desperation and longing.

Since we took two cars, I sent Charlie, Peter, and Naomi on home with all the crap we'd brought with us. The girls, still eating cobbler, wanted their walk along the lake—what I'd promised to keep Mallory close for the last half hour.

"We'll be fine," I said, looking away from Charlie's stricken face. I spooned cobbler into Anna's mouth; Mallory was eating it straight from the baking dish, her lips and chin a smear of blue crumbs.

He hesitated.

"I'm coming home," I said. "Don't worry."

He picked up Mallory's bike. Yellow plastic tassels fluttered from the handlebars. We hadn't let Mallory zoom down the hill after all. She wanted to go alone. But who would see her furious pedaling, her knees moving like pistons through the long grass? Who would see her in enough time if she was moving, too? She needed a larger body, the bigger target running beside her, ready to grab her ponytail, the hood of her sweatshirt, any small thing to make her stop. Charlie had insisted.

She crossed her arms. "I hate you, Daddy."

"Okay," he had said. "Okay. Okay," he said again, as if to steady himself. "Hate me. But no one's getting hurt today."

Peter and Naomi waited at the bottom of the hill. In one hand, Naomi held the picnic basket; in the other, the three bottles of wine, a finger plugged into each neck. Peter had the chairs and tray table.

I sighed. "Really. Go. Fifteen minutes and we'll be right behind you."

Fifteen minutes and we were still poking around in the reeds trying to stir up a frog. It was growing dark and things were going gray. The frogs were all around us. Thok! Thok! Thok! But nothing jumped out.

I shifted Anna to my hip. She was sleepy and wrapped her hands around my neck, rested her head into my shoulder. "Two more minutes," I said. "Anna has to get to bed and we have to get home to Daddy."

"No, we don't," Mallory said, then squatted and pushed her hands around the mucky grass. "We can stay here forever and nobody would ever know. They'd think we ran away."

She stood up, triumphant, her hands cupped together, peering into the open space between her thumbs.

"Now what do I do," she asked, her hands held up to me. Inside, the smallest of frogs absolutely still except for its yellow throat which puffed in and out.

"It's up to you," I said.

Slowly, as if they were hinged together, she opened her hands. The frog was green with black splotches, no bigger than her palm which was not big at all. She stroked its head, then curled her fingers around it.

"Momma," she said suddenly, pointing over my shoulder, "someone's coming."

I expected Charlie, his hands buried in his pockets, worried that we hadn't come home yet, that they'd been waiting all this time in the parking lot listening to the radio. That Peter and Naomi had asked what was wrong with us: Debra too quiet, Charlie too loud. That maybe they were just projecting because god knows they were having difficulties themselves, trying and failing to get pregnant for the past year and all. That Charlie had said *no*, everything was fine, when he meant *yes*, it was shit. That Charlie had said *yes*, it was shit, when he meant *no*, it was fine. That he was coming back to get me, and that was that. No more talk about leaving or separation or needing space.

But it was the dirt bike kid lurching towards us in a tidy blue sweater and clean chinos, his hands buried in his pockets, and his red hair combed in place, still shower-damp. I hugged Anna close; Mallory clutched her frog to her chest.

"He's back," Mallory said.

"I see," I said, though of course, I couldn't.

He held out his hand. "I wanted to apologize again. The right way."

I shook his hand. It was warm, friendly.

"If I'd known anyone was up there at all, I never would have gone that way." He wasn't a kid: he wasn't twenty but he wasn't twelve. And he was taller than me. "I mean," he said, "I shouldn't have been up there at all." He waited, smiled tentatively at Mallory who smiled back.

It was obvious he'd gone straight home, had imagined the worst. What was that for him? Jail? License suspended? The state police showing up at dinner that night, his father whacking him across the face? *Damn it kid, why do you have to be so stupid?*

What could I say that would equal his apology? That I was sorry, too? That he, like me, would now carry the burden of the almost-dead? The near miss? Those are the consequences, kiddo. Live with them.

He was looking hard at Mallory, then at Anna huddled against me. Maybe he got the scare of his life: he saw my girls crushed under his muddy tires and it would keep him up until the empty hours of the night thanking his god that what could have so easily happened, didn't. As I'd had mine: her cold body at the bottom of a ravine.

But then Mallory was crying, her hands open, the frog poised in its dumb patience, waiting to be set free. "Momma, look. Its leg is gone. Something chopped it off."

She was right. Its thin back leg ended at what looked like its knee. Nipped off by a crow? By a fish when it was still a tadpole? Another frog? How it hopped, how it had survived this long was anyone's guess. "Maybe you should put it back," I said.

Already though, she had tipped it into the boy's hand. He bent down close to her. "I don't think anything happened to him," he said. "He was probably born this way which means he's a pretty tough customer."

Mallory was skeptical.

"Really," he said, and handed back the frog. "My dad's a biologist at the college. He studies frogs. A whole bunch have been showing up like this over the past few years."

"A mutation?" I asked.

"A deformation," he said. "Not from genes, though. My dad thinks it's probably agricultural runoff. Pesticides or something."

I didn't have the heart to tell him that Charlie taught at the college, too, that he probably knew his father. The kid had come back of his own volition, ready to face the four of us and our righteous anger. How could he know what we would do? We'd been drinking, after all. And Charlie with that wine bottle. We might insist he give us his name, his address, his life savings. Or drag him through the mud, force feed him tofu, cut out his heart. He came back and he was sorry and I believed him.

"You're taking him home?" he asked.

Mallory nodded, cupping her hands tight again.

"How far is home?"

"Ten minutes," I said.

"If you follow me to the parking lot, I've got a bucket in my car. You need to keep him wet." He knelt back down next to Mallory, his knee sinking into the ground, his hand on her shoulder. "He breathes through his skin, so if his skin dries out, he'll die. But you'll take good care of him, right?"

Mallory smiled, leaned shyly into my side but I was trembling because when he turned his hand over, resting it on Mallory's shoulder, I saw what he had done.

Knuckles swollen, each one scraped deliberately, newly raw. And at his side, his other hand. That, too. No careless fall from the motorcycle after our earlier meeting, no accidental brush against the terrible bark of a tree, but something hard and unforgiving and still and deliberately in the way. The stuccoed wall of a house or a stack of cinder blocks punched down one by one.

"Just remember," he was saying, "once you take him home, that means he'll need you to do everything for him. Water, food, grass for a bed. But maybe without you, he wouldn't make it out here for much longer. The birds start storing up for winter and frogs are easy pickings."

When he stood up, he must have seen my eyes on his hands because he gave me a pinched, desperate smile and slid them into his pockets.

There was nothing I could say.

Later that night, after Mallory settled the frog into his new home (a plastic container, a saucer full of water, some rocks from the garden), after Peter and Naomi went to bed (early, finally; we'd be off at seven to take them to the airport), after Charlie went to bed (alone, under protest), I sat in the kitchen in the dark, listening to Anna through the monitor, her rustle of breath. Then I switched it off and listened to the house and its silence, trying to imagine what it would be like without the three of us here. The refrigerator hummed, the heat kicked on and off, in the distance, a dog barked, and then Charlie thumped down the stairs.

"It's dark," he said.

"Yes," I said.

"Are you coming to bed?" he asked, his hands waiting on the back of my chair.

"I don't know," I said. "Not yet."

"But soon?"

I nodded. When he left, I switched the monitor back on. The silence was unbearable.

Zorya

I could have just sucked him off and none of the trouble would have started, but then, there would have been no end to the trouble.

I was hanging sheets to dry in the early morning sun behind the hotel, the wind off the sea whipping them in my face. Cyclops, the one-eyed stray cat who'd taken to following me around, was beside the laundry basket flicking his tail. Stavros was suddenly behind me, waiting, his shadow on me as I struggled to pin the thin sheets to the line.

"You know, Zorya," he finally said, as I reached into the basket for another wet bundle, "there's another way to make money to send home."

I wrung the sheet between my hands, squeezing out rinse water, knowing what was coming, because it was what always came from men like him. Already, he'd taken up with Olena, who'd made the leap from maid service to waitress at the pool café, serving soggy food and overpriced coffee to big-bellied Germans. She no longer slept in the narrow room we shared behind the laundry room. Stavros bought her miniskirts and stilettos, which she wobbled on while carrying trays of food from the kitchen to the tables. She made sure to shake her mini-skirted ass for the foreign men in their tiny swim suits. But drunks on vacation are always stingy.

"I'm fine with money," I said, and shook the sheet.

"But you could use more," he said. "Easy money. You give me blowjobs, I give you money."

I pinned a corner of the sheet to the line, closed my eyes and took a deep breath: sea and salt, dust and thyme, lemons, and somewhere close by, garbage rotting in the heat.

His hand slipped around my waist and his fingers pressed into my stomach. "All you pretty Russian girls do this back home. Don't pretend you don't. You come here wanting to make money for the summer, so make money."

"Ukrainian," I said. "Not Russian."

"All the same," he said.

I squirmed, dropped the wet sheet into the dirt, and said nothing. Stavros finally walked away, muttering his curses. I gathered another sheet in my hands and pressed the damp cloth to my face. There was a time I would have said "yes" without hesitation. But not now. The money I sent home to my mother and Fedir had to be clean, free of shame.

Then Cyclops was rubbing his body around my feet, pushing an insistent nose against my skin. One vacant socket, one dark eye narrowed at me, most of his left ear bitten off, his orange and brown fur matted in clumps, his body rangy and bony.

● ● ●

I was alone on Naxos Island, working at Hotel Dionysus because of Fedir, who was in Kharkiv with my mother. Before, it was Hotel Zeus in Athens for two years, and before that the Dynamite! Hostel for eight months, which meant I hadn't seen Fedir for two years and ten months, which made my son five years and eight months old.

He would not recognize me, wouldn't know to call me Mama even if I sent all I earned back home so my own Mama could keep the apartment on Artema Street, so there'd be food in the refrigerator, so Fedir could have new winter clothes that fit him, covering his long arms and legs, covering his wrists and ankles from the biting wind and driving cold, so he could have swimming lessons on Saturday mornings in the ugly, freezing public natatorium because he didn't have a father like I had, who could teach him on Sundays how to swim freestyle and backstroke and breaststroke and even butterfly in the clear, still lake in the middle of the pine forest in Vovchansk, and when shivering and goose pimpled, a mother who waited on the grass with towels, a blanket spread across the pine needles, and a hamper packed with sausage, cheese, and poppy seed cake and the father and the mother and the child flopped on their backs in the afternoon sunshine, arms and legs bumping against each other, sticky pine needles twirling down in the breeze, tangling in their hair.

This is what I tell myself when I am scrubbing the shit and piss from the toilets two thousand four hundred and thirteen miles away from him. All those Euros sent by money transfer had to be worth it. Had to be, or else what was I?

A group of American women were at the hotel for some strange meeting. A pamphlet in a guest rooms said: "Resurrecting Your Goddess." The women held hands and chanted every morning at sunrise on the beach, then read their lives out loud in a circle beneath the shade of the tamarisk tree a few yards from the laundry line, trying to be heard over the cicadas. They sat atop small mats in the dirt, twisted in various nervous postures: crossed-legged, hands-wrapped-around-knees, arms gripped around stomachs. A circle of pain. In the evenings, they took turns hitting little cymbals and lying flat on their backs in the circle's center while the teacher moved her hands across their bodies and chanted *Hola Molykowa Eee Tramydos*. Nonsense words.

The teacher, a ponderous middle-aged woman, dressed in long, flowing kaftans and ugly, plastic sandals, sat above the women on a café chair. Her arms jangled stacks of noisy bracelets, which sent Cyclops running for cover every time she shambled by. Her hair was shockingly white, unkempt, and hung to her hips like a wooly poncho. But her acolytes were captivated, happily jogging back and forth to refill her water. They had individual meetings on her room's balcony where the women often sobbed as the teacher read aloud from their notebooks.

If only they knew what a slob and a sham she was in private. In her room, a trail of sticky syrup and shredded phyllo led from counter to couch to pillow. A half-eaten peach rotted on the table covered with tiny ants. Empty wine bottles at her bedside. Clothes scattered on the floor, wet towels thrown on the bed, the shower drain plugged up with tangled nests of her white hair.

As I hung the sheets and pillowcases and towels, I overheard bits of what the students read from their notebooks to the group—*I cannot say it with beautiful language: my father raped me when I was ten*—*I held the shell to my ear, heard the rush of the ocean, and wanted to drown*—*When my husband returned from Afghanistan after his second tour of duty, he locked himself in the bathroom, wrapped himself in the plastic shower liner, and shot himself*—*What is left? The ravaged body, the scars, the wasteland.*

Why did they want the teacher's assessment of their pain? What did she know about sponging up what is left of a husband from the grout of bathroom tiles? What did she know about bruises on your thighs? What would she ever know about cleaning rooms in Hotel Cosmopolit in Kharkiv, leaving the university because my father died of lung cancer and my mother could only sit in a chair in the dark corner of her room and stare out the window? I had to earn money to pay rent and buy groceries and keep the heat going in the winter, but that money wasn't enough, so I made it known to foreign businessmen—Italian, Chinese, German—and older men only, not younger men who might make ugly demands, and not Ukrainian men who would only show contempt for me or refuse to pay me or hit me—that I would be willing to offer extra services. They didn't refuse.

By older men, I meant men with gray in their hair, wrinkles and jowls, men happy just for a straightforward fuck. And because Cosmopolit was one of the premier hotels in Kharkiv, and because most of these men were traveling alone for only a few days, they didn't want trouble, just wanted to fulfill their fantasy of sex behind the (now defunct) Iron Curtain. And look how easy I made it! No need to go to cheap discos or back alleys or deal with slick pimps. I'd even change the sheets and make the beds afterwards.

I was careful, but not careful enough. I got pregnant and waited and worried for all those months. What if my child was a son, which father would he look like? What if he didn't look like his father but my father? My father, who used to sneak me into the airplane factory on Saturday nights where he was a wiring installer for the Antonov An-2 Colt, a plane holding the world record for having been in production the longest—forty-five years—and for twenty years, my father worked on those planes for nine hours a day, five days a week, missing only three days of work in all that time: the day I was born, the day my mother had a miscarriage and had to have a hysterectomy, and the day he underwent the tests that came back positive.

When I was a child, my father would flash his identity card at the night watchman, who couldn't have cared less that a little girl was hiding under the front flap of his overcoat if he handed over a little money. In the dark hanger, the planes were lined up like enormous, skeletal birds. My father would climb into one and hoist me up and we'd sit at the controls. "Okay. Tonight we aim for Alaska, Timbuktu, Java, Kathmandu." My father was always well-armed with information. His destinations never random, but researched in advance.

"Coordinates: 30° South, 91° West. The Galapagos Islands. Marine iguanas, sea lions, blue-footed boobies, flightless cormorants, the waved albatross, and flamingos."

I sighed happily. To leave our small apartment and bitter winter for a blue-footed boobie? "Aye Aye, Captain," I said.

When Fedir was born, he looked nothing like my father, nor anyone I knew. But later, when I received photographs from my mother, when Fedir was older, then older, then older, I could see my father: Fedir at the park, hanging from the climbing bars, his face tipped towards the sky and the drifting clouds, and laughing. There, there was my father.

A guest knocked on the bathroom door while I was scrubbing the shower, as if it was my room and not hers.

"Ramona," she said, "or Eos."

I shook my head, not understanding what she meant.

She was in a bright orange bikini, her brown hair bobbed, her face inside parentheses. She was thin, her skeleton visible beneath her skin—clavicle and ribs, hipbones and wrist bones, cheekbones and even, it seemed, the contours of her skull. Mama would prescribe a regime of *solyanka* soup, rich with sausage, cabbage, and hunks of bread to sop up the fatty broth. She would scare the ghost from Ramona's body.

Ramona continued, "It's what Judith, Gaia, calls me. We all have goddess names."

I shook my head again, took her outstretched hand. "I am Zorya." Or *Ilithia*, Idiot, what Stavros called me when I made mistakes.

"You aren't Greek," Ramona said.

"No. I am from Ukraine."

She leaned against the doorway. "That's a long way to come to clean my room."

I shrugged. "The money is better here. You, too, come a long way, no?"

"Back in the United States, Judith is the real deal. You know, famous, on television, and she wrote a book about growing up on a yoga commune. Love, enlightenment, and karmic attunement. But the guru liked little girls, you know, a pedophile? Her parents knew about it, but he was the guru."

I understood *television* and *yoga* and *pedophile* but not a father who could give his daughter away like that, which is why the teacher might arm herself with jangly bracelets and call herself a goddess. A goddess never sucked dick on demand.

"So," I said, "she is your writing teacher?"

"I'm boring by comparison. Ordinary, anyway. I teach in New York City. Kids are chauffeured to school and the cafeteria serves organic Nuggets. You know, like McDonald's only made with beans? We practice loving-kindness and kids assert their 'energetic forces' which we 'creatively redirect.' My story? Last year, my husband slipped in front of a subway an hour after he'd been fired."

Odd to be talking about this across the toilet. If I leaned over, I could kiss her. She must have been angry having to say, "Good Morning Children!" with her insides twisted. My insides were twisted, too. My son was five years and eight months old. I had not seen him in two years and ten months.

"My story is I must finish scrubbing shower or else hotel man not pay me," I said. Money, not pain, was the only reason I was here.

That night, I sat on the bed beneath the dim light, smacking at mosquitoes, my palm smeared with blood. Scattered around me were Fedir's drawings—monsters, snowmen, and stick figures holding hands—and photographs of Fedir—as an infant and toddler, the years I was present, and three and four and five, the years I was gone. I did not do this often because when I did, I lost resolve, more each time, incrementally weakened: go home to Fedir and go back to fucking old men. This weakness, love's agonies, was why I kept the papers and photographs bundled at the bottom of my suitcase and only called home twice a year.

I could earn more if I said "Yes" to Stavros. Certainly, it would mean a better room, one free of mosquitoes; Olena would be moved back to cleaning and laundry, and I would be elevated to the café. But I am not that person anymore. I am the person I was once before, the person my father hoped I would become.

"Zorya," my father had said, interrupting a poem I was reading, his thin hand grasping for mine. He was four days from death. "You must not sacrifice the dignity of your dreams for convenience."

I squeezed his hand. "But you wanted to be a pilot?"

A faint laugh. "No, I would have made a terrible pilot. Maybe a research scientist. But even if I had the money for university, they wouldn't have let me leave the country. You don't have that to stay. You are free."

"Yes" to Stavros would have been convenient. The only possible answer was "No."

How did I make up for my absence? How did I prove this difficult love even if Fedir would never know? I said "No" to everything but work, allowing myself only a few hours' sleep, and the meals provided by the job, or the rotting fruit on sale, the day-old bread at the bakery, the leftovers in the cabinets and refrigerators of the hotel guests—tins of sardines, half packages of macaroni, stale cookies. "No" to all pleasure. When a Ukrainian friend wanted to see the Acropolis? "No." When the hotel staff went out dancing? "No." When Olena wanted to go to a bar at the port and flirt with anyone willing to buy her drinks? "No." When the sea called me to wade in, to dive into the cold water, to swim back and forth across the bay? "No. No. No." I was here to work and send money home, not choose convenience over dignified resolution. How could I be my father's daughter with Stavros' dick in my mouth for a few Euros in my palm? I was here now so I could return to Fedir and take him wherever he wanted to go.

Ramona was staring at her notebook when I walked into her room, her face pinched.

"I start in the bathroom?"

"It doesn't matter," she said. "You aren't interrupting anything. I've been writing the same thing over and over: 'Fuck you. Why did you leave me?' As if his ghost will answer. That's all I have and I'm supposed to read this in two days."

I planted the broom into the floor like a stake. "If you keep asking question and asking question, then you must write answer. Write question, write answer. Write question, write answer. Maybe you not find his answer or right answer, but you search and not just wait."

Ramona eyed me head to toe, and then smiled. "Brilliant. There is more to your story than cleaning toilets."

I said, "I was in university for two years. I study English. My father die. My mother sit by window and stare at road, at snow, at everything gray and ending. I leave University. No money. I start cleaning and have Fedir, my son, and now I send money to him. The rest you know." I said all of this very fast because my life before my other work was a life that promised other possibilities no longer mine.

"I'm sorry," Ramona said. "How did your father die?"

"Lung cancer."

He had refused to go back to the hospital in the end. Instead, we arranged a bed on the couch, his bottle of pain pills on the side table, and Mama and I took turns nursing him. His breathing rattled and choked, his legs too weak to stand on, so we used diapers and changed him right there, trying to be quick, knowing if he still had his senses, he would find this an assault on his dignity. My father, not a religious man, suddenly calling "God help me!" when the pain came. When he was awake, I read to him, poetry, Pushkin: *And here they come - a ghostly swarm of guests, my long-lost friends, the fruits of all my dreams.* My father, Papa, whispered, "Again, again."

"How do you bear it? Separated from your son?" she asked.

"I start on bathroom," I said, in answer. "Mop at end."

Ramona nodded. "You should swim. Gaia says bad spirits are attached to us, holding on to us, but when we dive under water, they drown and when we come up for air, we're free. Maybe bullshit, but the water clears my head."

I was stripping the teacher's bed when Stavros barreled in. Once again, a variety of stains stippled the sheets—something like wine, definitely coffee, maybe peach juice, a smear of fuchsia lipstick, a smudge of black eyeliner.

Stavros ran his finger along the edge of the counter, then swiped it around the sink.

"Bravo," he said, "But the bed is not complete? You are behind." His hair was slicked back with shiny gel, like a mobster. Olena's doing.

"Everything but bed." He brushed my hair from my shoulders, and then gripped my neck. "So pretty with some nice clothes and makeup. More beautiful than Olena. You could be my cafe girl if 'Yes.'"

I shrugged.

"Think," he said, tapping my forehead, "but not too long. Many girls want this work. Many girls who say 'Yes.'"

When he left, I sat on the bed for many minutes, but did not cry.

A fierce wind had kicked up, blowing pine needles and dust and pink flower petals along the stairs and paths around the hotel. Stavros said to sweep it all up, but it was impossible. I'd clear an area and fifteen minutes later clear it again.

Olena clickety-clacked down the stairs. Bright purple heels, some sort of spandex dress, and cheap clusters of fake gold balls knocking against each other around her neck. Her hair was now blond.

"Poor Zorya," she crooned. "So hot and windy. You look like shit."

"It's no matter," I said.

Olena leaned into the railing, ran her fingers through her hair, letting the strands fall slowly back to her shoulder. "Stavros took me to the salon. He likes blond Russians."

"But you're Ukrainian."

"What do I care? Russian, Ukrainian. Once we were all one country. My pussy, I dyed myself. Do you want to see?" She began to pull up her dress.

"No, Olena."

A pout as she dropped the hem and then glared. "You think Stavros will feel sorry for you and hold you while you cry about your son, and maybe he will begin to kiss you, and then he is yours?"

I shook my head. "No. Stavros is yours."

She clickety-clacked closer. Her perfume smelled of crushed roses. "You cannot compete. You," she said, and pinched my tee-shirt away from my chest and then let it fall back, "a shuffling, sweaty, old Baba. Stay away." She patted my cheek and left.

Desperation. Who knew what Stavros demanded in bed? If he didn't discard Olena for me, it would be some other girl from Bucharest or Murmansk or Kiev, easily perfected with spandex and spiked heels and hair dye.

And Olena? What she told me in the room behind the laundry was that her parents died in a car crash when she was very young, and so she was raised by her grandparents on a farm in Podolia where they tended cherry trees. Their machinery was outdated and then two disastrous harvests—late freezes, no blossoms on the trees, and just like that, they were forced to sell the farm and moved into a small apartment where Olena slept on a couch.

One after the other, her grandparents died. "Broken hearts," she said. "They couldn't see across the valley into their trees, just the concrete apartment tower, narrow hallways, six floors of stairs and an elevator that never worked. The ugly forest of these gray buildings—all of that stopped their hearts." So, Olena sold mobile phones, found two roommates to help pay the rent, but then she was fired: the manager insisted she use her lunch breaks to fuck him. She refused and eventually found her way here, where she decided not to refuse any more.

I couldn't sleep: mosquitoes whined at my ears, cats yowled out on the road, and the Germans were drunk, singing and laughing on their patio. I dressed, walked to the beach, and sat under the stars. The sea was as still as the skating rink at Dzerzhinsky square where my father would take me when the moon was bright and my mother asleep. He'd sit on the cold benches under lamplight and study his airplane operating manuals, or watch me skate laps around the rink, my blades catching in the grooves left by daytime skaters.

When my fingers and toes burned with cold, I'd sit beside him on the bench while he smoked. He'd say, "In this, we refuse to live like machines, repeating the same tasks every day, dreaming the same dreams every night. Don't you feel as if anything is possible, Dochka? Gliding like a swan under the moon? This is the hour for flight." He would untie my skates and ease them from my frozen feet, and then he would take each foot and rub them between his hands.

What was Fedir dreaming about now? The caged lion at Gorky Park? Me, his Mama, a sliver of my face cut from a photograph? Or perhaps my mother was stroking his forehead, quieting his night terrors, singing a lullaby.

In the distance, I heard laughter and splashing. Two people holding hands, walking at the edge of the sea. I sat back in the shadows, hugged my knees to my chest, and suddenly, as they stepped into the light, I saw that it was the teacher and Stavros; she'd gathered her kaftan and held it high at her broad hips, and he'd rolled his pants to his knees. Even so, they were both still wet: the teacher's long, white hair coiled in a rope down her back; Stavros, bare-chested. In his free hand, he held towels.

They paused before coming up the path to the hotel, and Stavros drew her against him, her bracelets jangling, and then they were kissing, locked together, his hand swimming across her ass, and when they finally broke apart, he gave a loud sigh.

"You are beautiful," he said. "A real woman, not like girls here who just want my money."

I was frightened they might put their towels down in front of me and held my breath, but they turned up the path and disappeared into the darkness.

Poor Olena.

• • •

The next morning, I was hanging sheets, while Cyclops wound himself around my legs, butting his head into my calves. His empty socket was infected, rimmed with crust and ooze. His ribs and spine were prominent; the bits of chicken and fish I took from the café's garbage cans were not making a difference. How long could he hold out? All the strays had some ailment—a gimpy leg or no leg at all, a missing ear or half a tail, festering sores or mangy fur.

Ramona was walking down the path in a long white shirt, her orange bikini a reverse shadow; her hands clutched her notebook. She adjusted the brim of her wide straw hat. "How do you stand this? It's unbearable."

I shrugged. "I have done worse."

"I brought my story," Ramona said. "Would you listen?"

"I have towels and then must return to clean rooms." I was suddenly angry. Three baskets of towels, twenty toilets and showers and sinks to scrub, and then beds to make and rooms to tidy, and then pathways and stairs to sweep. And really, was her scribbling in between swims in the Aegean truly work? Even Cyclops worked harder, scrounging in dumpsters, hunting mice, fighting off disease and exhaustion. And wasn't it a kind of indulgence, using a two week vacation to tell what has already happened? There was nothing more to know. Her husband cannot answer her. Meanwhile, Fedir was struggling in the pool to stay afloat, to swim to the other end, his arms and legs flailing with fatigue, his swim instructor yelling for him to Push Harder! Fedir wishing he had a Mama encouraging him when he reached the deep end, where she would scoop him from the water and hold his shivering body against hers.

But Ramona had already put her notebook on the ground, seized a basket, and was hanging towels on the line. "I'll help," she said, and gave a wide smile.

"Okay." Maybe her writing the question and answer could help her return home to the silly, uncomplicated love of her students, to their paper hearts and flowers, and their tiny hands tugging at her.

We worked quickly and then sat in the shade beneath a plane tree. Ramona took off her hat and cleared her throat.

She took a deep breath.

"Q: Why the fuck did you leave me?

"A: I didn't mean to. I was at the platform edge and I was only considering the possibility and I was jostled and fell.

"Q: Why did you leave me?

"A: I was fired and then, I was on the tracks.

"Q: Why did you leave me?

"A: I wasn't leaving you. I was leaving me."

Ramona closed the notebook. "There's more—it goes in a different direction."

I leaned my head against the tree trunk, studied the feathery leaves, the dappled sky behind them. The same sky above Fedir.

Q: Why did you leave me, Mama?

A: For the money, you see? I won't be gone forever.

Q: Why did you leave, Mama? I am old enough to know.

A: I couldn't be a good Mama for you.

Q: Are you coming back? Are you looking at the sky like I am?

"So?" Ramona was waiting.

"Yes," I said. "Good. Sad. True."

She hugged me.

I looked up: Olena stood on the patio above the laundry lines, her blond hair shimmering, her body girdled in black spandex, her hands on her hips. Of course, she would tell Stavros.

Ramona waved. Olena waved back. "She works at the café, right? She's nice, friendly, always refilling my water. She's like you? From the Ukraine, too?"

"Yes, like me," I said. "But I am not much like her now."

• • •

Did it matter when I told Stavros that the guest spoke to me first? Put her arms around me first? That Ramona insisted on helping me with the laundry? No. Rules were rules. Guests were not friends. Did it matter that I did my job and left the rooms clean? That the towels and sheets were dry and removed from the line by noon so as not to offend the guests with an obstructed view of the beach? No. Olena had registered several complaints from guests: sandy floors, filthy toilets, and dirty sheets. Did it matter that I always gathered spare coins into a pile by the bedsides or scattered jewelry in saucers on the dressers? No. Did it matter that I needed this job even though it didn't pay much, even though I worked from sunrise to sunset, even though it meant separation from my son? No. If I really needed this job, if I really loved my son, then why have I not said "Yes"?

In order to receive my pay, I had to finish out the day, and then leave. When I pleaded that there was no ferry back to Athens until the next morning, Stavros shrugged and said, "This is not my problem. It is yours."

Now, I sit on top of my suitcase at the beach waiting out the night with the enormous moon, counting stars, listening to the push and pull of the waves against the shore. My skirt and shirt and underclothes are folded on top of a white towel, the hotel's, a small theft, but I need something for sleep. I walk to the water's edge, squish my toes into the coarse sand. No one else but me. I listen to my father, a ghost standing beside me, standing inside me, speaking to me, a ghost I will not wash away.

"Enough," he says. "Your son is waiting: maybe you will surprise him, arrive in the dark of night, slip beside him in bed, your body fitting itself to his and he will awaken to you, his Mama; or maybe it will be day and he will be at the playground, ready to launch himself down the slide, and you will run to the bottom, ready to catch him. You don't know that he loves the slide, pretends it is a secret tunnel to a cave filled with pirate's treasure. You don't know he has learned to pump his legs, swinging higher and higher so his toes skim the leaves of the linden tree. You don't know because when you left him, he was knocking down blocks and banging a wooden spoon on the pots and pans."

And then he is gone and I am speaking only to myself.

The ferry comes in thirteen hours, which means in the morning I will need to find shade. Or won't. Instead, I'll wade into the water—ankles, then legs, then hips, then under. When Fedir touches my sunburned skin, he will wonder if I am fire. When he picks cockles and whelks from my knotted, briny hair, he will wonder if I am water. When he sees my bruises, he will wonder how I escaped the terrible pirates and I will tell him that when their ships closed in, I dove under the sea, holding my breath for hours and days, then surfaced, swimming for home because he, my son, was waiting for me. Or not. Maybe I was a ghost he wouldn't know to remember. Maybe he will wonder if I was only ever air.

Survival of the Fittest

My God, it is intolerable to think of spending ones whole life, like a neuter bee, working, working, & nothing after all.—One cannot live this solitary life, with groggy old age, friendless & cold, & childless staring one in ones face, already beginning to wrinkle.
    –Charles Darwin, "The Pros and Cons of Marriage," 1838

At "Pretty! Pretty! Nails," Eliza tries to relax into the vibrating massage chair while staring at the stone Buddha on the floor. If only she could concentrate with his same clarity on her own mucked-up life, but the chair's mechanical fists pummel her kidneys, and toxic fumes distract her focus. Almost all the salon employees are Vietnamese, recent immigrants. She tries to over-tip since their hourly wage can't be a living wage, hoping for sixty minutes of mostly uninterrupted silence excepting the necessary "Round? Square? Pick a color? You Pay Now?"

All she asks for is an hour and then back home to Steve and the conversation started but not finished. He was off again to Thailand for the semester, mating season for his bats, another chance to be the first to record them on film doing their bat business while she stayed behind with their daughter. Bumblebee bats, the world's smallest mammals, barely an inch and weighing less than a penny, wrecking balls through their marriage.

"Eliza! Are you awake?"

She opens her eyes and Audrey Stone and her daughter, Avery, are lowering themselves into the massage chairs beside her, both in tennis whites, still dewy at the temple. The inter-club tennis season is a blood sport. The victors' names inscribed on a silver-plated cup. Eliza wants nothing to do with that scene. Or any scene. How do you do scenes? Or enter scenes? Or stage scenes? Really, the only thing she knows, according to Steve, is how to make a scene. But only when it matters. When Steve's work matters more than their marriage. When his graduate students matter more than their daughter. When the reproductive cycles of his Bumblebee bats matter more than their own sex life. Things between them are wrong, terribly wrong, perhaps irreparably wrong, but she doesn't know how to fix them or their daughter, or in what order, or if she can. Steve had retreated to the safety of his lab and quantifiable research. The last time she felt his hand on the small of her back? Or resting on her knee while watching a movie, the weight of his hand holding her down, claiming her in that way? Sure, they weren't so far gone that they didn't fuck now and then, but it was mechanical, efficient, without intensity. Without need. Anyone else would probably do.

Audrey sighs in the direction of her daughter who is furiously texting. "You know what it's like. Oh," she says, and reaches across the great divide between the massage chairs, and rests her fingers on Eliza's forearm.

Avery holds her phone to her chest, thumbs at full stop, waiting, it seems, to hear what her mother will say.

Audrey says, "I'm sorry about Hannah, what happened at the party. The drugs. Of course, if boys were saying those things about me when I was that age—or did those things—I mean, I don't blame her—well. It makes sense in the moment." She reaches over with her other hand and pats her daughter on the arm.

Avery offers up a sweet, nauseating, sympathetic smile.

Eliza can't, won't hear anymore. Long pounds the bottoms of her feet with his fists. She would like to bolt from "Pretty! Pretty! Nails" right now, but that would mean making a scene. Hannah. She had been the one to discover her daughter's hair-spray bottle filled with vodka, and the angry cuts and scars hidden on her forearm under the stack of woven bracelets. What does Audrey know that she doesn't know? Hannah passed out in a back bedroom? Forced to vomit the pills into a toilet? Did someone take photos of her passed out? Or worse? Because that's what kids did now—some kids.

She nods at Audrey while looking at the Buddha behind the ziggurat of oranges. His eyes are closed, his hands relaxed, and his mouth curved in a smile that suggests, by extension, if she believes in peace, love and forgiveness, she'll be okay. All of them okay. But she doesn't believe this. Because when she turns to look at Avery, she knows that if Audrey wasn't here, she'd slap her. Avery. One of the girls responsible for her daughter's misery. One of the girls who posted photos of Hannah drunk, with a boy.

Pills. She wants to puke into the foot basin. She wants to hurl the Buddha against the wall. Shatter his serene heart. Long is still painting her toenails and there is still topcoat and then fifteen minutes under the dryer.

She pretends to answer her phone, pretends to talk into it. "Yes," she says, "right away. I'm coming." She takes out her wallet. "Here," she says, and hands Long forty dollars. "I'm sorry. I have to go." She pulls on her flip-flops, smearing the red polish across her toes.

She runs from the car to the back door, certain she is going to find Hannah on the bedroom floor and that running might reclaim seconds and save her, but Hannah is at the table eating an English muffin with peanut butter, pointing at her father's computer.

"Right there is where the baby attaches to the mother, right?" she says. "At the nipple? Even in flight it hangs on." She is not saying this to her father, who is flipping through a stack of papers, but to another woman, the new graduate assistant she assumes, likely the latest Thailand expedition assistant, likely the latest threat-who-is-not-a-threat-to-a-marriage-already-dead assistant.

Steve says, "Everything okay?"

Eliza shakes her head.

"Mom!" Hannah stares at her feet.

Steve leans over. "What the hell happened?"

The woman has a bleached-blonde, pixie haircut that only looks chic when a person is angular and underweight, though not anorexic, so almost impossible to pull off, and yet she does. The woman says, "That doesn't look good."

Eliza thinks of the Buddha's composure, his stony silence. "Nail polish," she says. "I'm fine."

"Did they use a nail gun?" Hannah says.

"I had to leave early. Non-emergency emergency," she says. "I'm Eliza, by the way," she says to the woman. She wants to say, 'Steve's wife,' but that would come across as territorial.

"Marcie," the woman says, and shakes her hand. "I'm Steve's assistant."

Marcie sits down and takes a long swig of beer. Four empty beer bottles on the counter. Not a lot, but more than nothing. While her husband and Marcie were drinking and talking bats, she was listening to Audrey Stone tell her how her daughter may or may not have overdosed on pills, how her daughter may or may not be trying to kill herself.

She listens to their talk now, behind her, as she stands at the sink washing out the beer bottles.

"You know," Hannah says, "that one bat can eat six hundred bugs in an hour?"

Eliza isn't sure if Marcie's "Wow" is genuine or meant to placate her daughter. But no matter. Hannah has more.

"Because that's the equivalent to one of us eating like twenty pizzas in one night, right? You or I'd be bulimic within a day. And you know how bats equal blood-sucking? In China, bats equal happiness and longevity. They even put little bat pins on babies. And in medieval times they'd burn you at the stake if bats flew over your house, but shamans believe that if you see a bat, you'll fly through the dark into the light. A cool reverse omen."

Hannah, so smart, raised on bats. Is that why she's a target? Beautiful, yes, but not shiny-smooth like the other girls, not adept at coded repartee. Steve used to bring Hannah to the lab on the weekends and she'd help with the bats, analyzing guano and running blood tests. They looked like little miniature, snub-nosed pigs, but Hannah called them "wood fairies." The bats would crawl down her arm to her fingertips and spread their wings for flight as if she was their tree. Then the university instituted new regulations—only approved personnel in the labs.

Hannah stayed out. They both stayed out.

They didn't always stay out. Before he switched over to the Bumblebees, Steve studied brown bats and echolocation. Easy to pack everyone up during summer afternoons and drive out to the woods and set up ultrasound microphones. She'd pack a picnic: a wedge of hard cheese, salami, a baguette, olives, sliced cucumber, a couple of peaches, and a turkey sandwich and Oreos for Hannah. They went on scavenger hunts, collecting feathers, moss, mushrooms, and once, a raccoon skull. As dusk settled, she and Hannah stretched across the blanket, flicking ants from their arms and legs while Steve tinkered with the equipment, and then they waited for the bats to fly in that heady, chattering rush for the sky. Sometimes Hannah fell asleep and they took turns hauling the equipment back to the car, and then Steve scooped Hannah up and against his body and Eliza walked behind them with the flashlight, illuminating trees and roots in their path, and she remembers thinking *when does this—us—end?*

She turns from the sink and puts the beer bottles in the recycling bin.

"No," Hannah says. "You can't just film them. Right, Dad? That why you have to go there?"

"Easy there," Steve says. He lowers his glasses to the tip of his nose. Moderator. "Marcie wasn't raised in a bat cave. She just crossed over from Screech Owls and into Bumblebees last month."

"Owls are cool," Hannah says. "We heard them all the time in the woods. But you can't set up a camera. You don't mess with the habitat of an endangered species."

"Got it," Marcie says, and takes a long swig of her beer. The landscape has shifted from easy camaraderie to teenage antagonism.

"It's not just a few wall-mounted cameras that disturb the mating pairs," Eliza says, wanting to be part of the conversation. "Isn't a main cause of their decline the monks meditating in their caves?" She looks at Steve, at the glasses on the tip of his nose, deliberate and far from the man who ran around with the microphone in the dark, immoderate not only in his love for the bats.

"Ironic, really," she says, "Buddhist monks as exterminators? I hope the bats shit on their bald heads." Do they nod? Does anyone say anything? She'd tried to smooth her anger into amiable indignation. No real ill-will for the monks merely, in their compassionate largesse, meditating on loving kindness—what was exactly absent in her inverse karmic curse. Hence, silence.

Marcie ruffles her white blonde hair, preening like a cockatoo. "I know, professional composure, but I can't believe we go to Thailand in two weeks. I only got as far as the Catskills with my owls."

"Marriage is really just survival of the fittest," her mother had once said to her from behind her large round sunglasses. She tipped her head down so that Eliza could see her eyes. Serious business. Late August and they were at the town pool: her mother sunned herself on the lounge chair like the other teacher-mothers on summer furlough; Eliza sat cross-legged on the ground, licking ketchup from french fries; and her father! He was here! He swam laps in the pool! Was this what her mother meant by fittest? Because her father was fit, strong, made of rippling muscles. She wasn't sure why he needed muscles for Wall Street, but he seemed to think they were necessary. Earlier, he'd summoned her to the pool's edge to count his laps. She grew bored and confused at forty-three and jumped in the water to practice underwater talking.

"You have to be prepared. You have to be your own woman." Her mother looked at her again over the lowered glasses. "Eliza, are you listening?"

She nodded vaguely, but what did her mother mean? She was ten. How could she be a woman? No boobs. No period.

Allowance every Sunday. The wavy heat from the concrete was making her woozy.

Her mother took off her glasses. "Listen to me. Don't give all of yourself away. Keep something in reserve."

That was how her mother survived her father and his relentless self-absorption. Her father wasn't unfaithful or reckless with money or alcoholic but he was an absent husband—no passion, no wooing, no affection. He loved himself, always buying the most expensive wool suits and his hair immaculately combed and his body perfectly fit. No love left for his wife, only benign regard.

Her mother watched her father flip turn then surface into his butterfly laps. "Remember," she said, "survival of the fittest is about who lasts the longest."

She scanned the medicine cabinet. Nothing immediately lethal, at least in small doses, but anything could damage in a large enough quantity. Maybe whatever Hannah had taken was hidden in her room. Maybe whatever she'd taken was gone.

Would some sort of inpatient program help? The psychiatrist said *not there yet* but now? Magic Mountain? Better in the Desert? Happy in the Clouds? Maybe the first step would be to ship off Audrey and Avery to Cannibal City where they could be eaten alive. She should check herself. That's what Steve said the last time they talked about Hannah. "Check yourself," he said. "Don't blow this out of proportion."

They were in the family room, on the couch, but nowhere near each other.

"I'm her mother," Eliza had said. "I have a right to be upset by this. Aren't you?"

Steve set his laptop on the coffee table. "We can have a measured response. Why give Facebook or Snapchat or whatever it is the time of day? Besides, Hannah doesn't care about what those kids think of her."

She was yelling. Maybe her fists were bunched. Maybe her response was unmeasured. "You know what they're saying. What they're writing. Kids kill themselves over these kinds of things."

"No," Steve said, "that's not Hannah. She hasn't given any indication of anything like that. Has she?"

"Are you going scientific method on me? She's not a bat or a frog or some invertebrate."

Suddenly Hannah was in the doorway, in her pajamas. "You know I can hear you all the way upstairs, right? That I'm not just a bunch of your comingled cells on a slide that you get to study. You don't get it, do you? Deal with your own shit and not mine." She turned and left.

They should have run after Hannah, holding her between them, though Hannah would have squirmed away. Instead, they sat on the couch in silence, listening to her thump up the stairs.

Finally, Eliza said, "To tell you the truth, I can't wait for you to go to Thailand. A trial run. Can we survive without you?"

"That's your truth?" Steve asked. "Our family isn't some Darwinian experiment."

She is lying on Hannah's bed staring at the ceiling: ceiling fan with its dusty white blades, a few scattered glow-in-the-dark sticker stars, a hairline crack that needed to be patched and painted. What else did Hannah see staring at her ceiling? Avery and her merry band of bitches, her father and her mother, some happier self?

Would telling Hannah about her own shame-filled adolescence help? The things you did or didn't do that make you want to disappear, dissolve, die?

The door opens and Hannah walks in. "What are you doing?"

Eliza sits up. "Talk?"

Hannah shrugs. "Then I go first." She sits at the foot of the bed. "Are you really going to let Dad go with that woman? Tell him you don't trust her. I don't. Do you know what she said to me? That she's lucky Dad didn't pick me for the Thailand trip."

"Look," Eliza says, "she's just nervous. Give her a chance. My turn." She swallows hard. She hadn't thought about the words. "I heard about the party." She watches Hannah as she says the next words. "That you took drugs. Too many. On purpose."

Nothing and then Hannah shakes her head, and then? She laughs. "I'm sorry. Not funny. But it is. Overdose? Suicide? I can see why you might believe that, but really? You think I would do something like that?"

Eliza is angry. "Really! I'm an idiot to think that you would do that? But you *have* done this." She holds Hannah's hand and pushes back her sleeve, expecting the old scars but not new, angry red cuts.

Hannah yanks her arm back.

"Why again?" Eliza says, flailing.

"Same reason you think I OD'ed," Hannah says.

"What about that?" Eliza says.

"There was no *that*. Let me guess. Avery?" Hannah's arm is behind her back. "You want the truth or the truth-truth?" Hannah says.

"Truth-truth," Eliza says. "All of it."

"The night I slept over at Avery's, she had this party and we did X, you know Ecstasy? After a few hours of feeling good, I passed out and nobody could wake me up. Avery and her friends threw me in the shower and I woke up. No suicide. Science experiment gone bad."

Her daughter's expression is both desperate and impassive. On the one hand, it could have been heroin. She's read about kids shooting up in the fancy suburbs. On the other hand, her daughter's arms have track marks of a different desperation. "You need to let me take care of this," she says, meaning Hannah's arm, but meaning Hannah.

She is looking at Steve as he is looking at his computer screen, tapping out notes. They sit at opposite ends of the couch. The cliché of any marriage that survives too long without sustained love and affection. Companionable silence, each giving the other all the space in the world, skimming the surface of each other's lives. Marriage of convenience because they are too tired to push through to anything more, so they settle for less. For better or worse. Waiting it out. She looks at Steve tapping at his keyboard. She knows that man sitting just a few feet away is the man she loves despite the graduate assistants, the bats, the lonely nights alone in bed.

But they can wait. Hannah can't.

She looks at Steve. "We need to do something before school starts. Before you leave."

Steve pauses his typing. "Outside of letting the school know about what's been going on, and contacting some of the kids' parents and her doctor?"

"Hannah won't let us do that," she says.

"Maybe we do it anyway. You think I don't see how seriously fucked up this is? That I don't see her? Or her arms, what you don't tell me about but what I see anyway?"

Eliza breathes in, then out. "I'm sorry. She wouldn't let me tell you. I didn't want to make any of this worse for her."

Steve moves over, beside her. "You're too far away for this."

Eliza rests her head on his lap. She is crying—it feels dangerous, like grief for something already lost.

They stay like that, close together, suspended in a kind of rapprochement. How easy is it to find your way back to someone? As simple as crawling across a couch? No. Though maybe it's a start because what is the alternative? Smash the Buddha? Shit on the monk? Survival of the fittest? Hadn't they survived together? Worse for the wear but still here, still tangled up with each other? Not the time to keep herself in reserve, but the time to spend herself with abandon.

Before they go to bed they are clear about what they will do: she and Hannah will go to Thailand and Marcie will return to her Screech Owls. Close ranks and tend to the wounded. Love is fierce in this way, mean and tribal under threat.

The doorbell is jarring and sudden, and then furious knocking at the door.

Steve runs down the stairs and she follows. No one is there. Just a car pulling away from the curb.

"I don't understand," she says, and checks her watch. 1:42 a.m. She flips on the porch light. A body on the lawn. Hannah.

"Hannah!" They both yell her name, they both run to her but Hannah is already sitting up, crying. Vomit on her shirt. "I'm sorry," she says.

Steve pulls her against him, strokes her hair. "It's okay," he says. "We'll clean you up."

Eliza holds her daughter's hand and panics. "Did you take anything?"

"Vodka. Enough to make it better," Hannah laughs a little and then cries.

"Make what better? What did you do?" She looks at Steve. "Please," she says to him. She doesn't know what else to say because she can see already from beneath the cuffs of her daughter's shirt sleeves that Hannah has cut herself again. Blood on her wrists and palms.

"You don't get it. I got fucked up so I could fuck a guy. Make all the shit they say about me true. Own it. So I did. But then after, I didn't want to. But how do you go back and not do what you did?"

Steve is whispering, his lips moving against Hannah's forehead. "It's okay it's okay it's okay."

She tugs Hannah's shirt off over her head and tosses it into the grass. She turns her daughter's arms over and runs her finger over the wounds. Nothing serious or deep, but of course it is serious and deep, through skin and bones to the heart. Steve is shaking his head. No way to spare any of them this pain. She slips out of her own shirt and helps Hannah into it, like dressing a small child—first the head, then one arm through a sleeve, then the other.

"I don't want to go inside," Hannah says. "Not yet."

"Then we won't," Eliza says. "We'll stay as long as you want."

They lie together on the lawn, their bodies close: Hannah's head is on Steve's chest and her hand in Eliza's. The grass sweet and damp and the night is quiet and still. Once upon a time, before everyone grew up and away and it all fell apart, they would lie on a blanket in the backyard staring at the stars. Steve studied a constellation chart—Orion, Ursa Major, Draco, Cassiopeia, Andromeda—and pointed at the heavens, tracing a line that started Here and went There, drawing a serpent or a swan.

Hannah raises her arm, which swerves unsteadily across the sky, tracking something high above the trees and then stops, "There." she says, "Do you see? Don't you see?"

Eliza and Steve don't yet see, because they are looking at Hannah's arm—the sleeve has crumpled to her elbow, and all those cuts are a constellation of pain. How can they look anywhere else?

But then they do.

A bat swoops through the pines behind the garage and then over the roof, circling the chimney, and then lighting off again for the trees. Swooping and circling, swooping and circling, swooping and circling over them.

Mourning, in Miniature

Striking resemblances never fail to perpetuate the tenderness of friendship, to divert the cares of absence, and to aid affection in dwelling on those features and that image which death has forever wrested from us.

–Charles Fraser, on Portrait Miniatures,
Charleston Times, May 27, 1807

His wife is starving. This realization is not an abstraction as in: starving for affection or love or sex. Or, if that is the case, then that consideration comes later. Nor is it a gradual, incremental illumination as in: each day less to hold, less heft, less left. It is that, too, but it is for now and most urgently a concrete fact. All night he'd been tossing and turning, so he inched up against Gemma, hoping her warmth and sleeping peace might settle him. Instead, when he tried to fit himself into her (knees inside knees, hips to hips, chest to back) and across her (arm over her shoulder, foot over foot), he felt absence and presence, hollow and gap, skin and bone.

He can see Gemma's body in the shadows but it is no longer a welcoming geography of hills and valleys, but an unforgiving geometry of angles and planes. Her spine is a knotted rope. And her waist. And her hip. And the side of her knee. He feels it all and wants to shake Gemma awake. Sleep is absurd. There's nothing left.

Instead, he thinks back over the day and their meals together.

She'd shrugged off breakfast. "Not now," she said, and bolted from the house for her five-mile run. Snowing and still running. To where? How fast? And really, how far? In this self-decimating fury, five miles could easily extend to ten. His negligence not to know. But he couldn't follow her, could never keep up anyway, not at his age, not with his paunch, and a car seemed perverse and dishonest—if she caught him.

Lunch. Roast beef and Swiss on rye. She'd slathered on the mustard and horseradish, but had she eaten any of it?

He'd been preoccupied with a new book: *Love and Loss: American Portrait Miniatures*. Gemma got up from the table, a napkin wadded in the middle of her plate.

"Slow poke," she said. "We'll never make the movie."

But the book. And that photograph of the brooch and the painting inside: *Harriet Goodridge, The Dead Daughter. December 1807-January 1808.*

Gemma feigned an exaggerated sigh and tapped her watch.

At the movies had she had any of the popcorn? Fistfuls. But then the crunch under his feet when he stood and then walked down the aisle.

Dinner: broiled salmon, green beans in garlic and olive oil, and an arugula and parmesan salad. He'd reached over with his fork, speared the rest of her fish. "No need to let it go to waste," he'd said.

But she was wasting away. That was evident. His beautiful wife. He never should have brought her the bones.

That baby painted in the brooch was dressed in a white gown and white bonnet, eyes closed, lashes sweeping her cheeks, tiny hands grasping, impossibly, a yellow daffodil in bloom. Who had worn that gold locket? Mother or Father? Pinned at the throat of a dress with the dead daughter inside? Or pinned to the interior lapel of a waistcoat? Regardless, open, shut, open, shut all day long. Beneath the brooch, this passage: "More than any other token of the time, the mourning miniature expressed the universal longing to keep the dead within the circle of the living."

He thinks of the dollhouse he is still building in the basement for the daughter who will never, now, be born. Originally, he'd imagined an un-dollhouse: unfussy, unstuffy, unconventional. Nothing like the kits—the austere Edwardian townhouses or finicky Gingerbread Victorians filled with teeny brass beds, five inch Turkish carpets, and finger-length Chippendale sofas. Nothing like the McMansions up in the gated development—great rooms with vaulted ceilings, gleaming stainless steel kitchens, espresso bars, spa bathrooms, and master suites with gas fireplaces.

What he'd imagined was a rambling one-level house built across hill and into rock and over water. He mapped it on graph paper, tabulated proportions, even rigged a prototype waterfall, but couldn't imagine a way to create half a home, couldn't see where to cut the structure in two so that it might hinge open for play. Where do you hide and seek in an open floor plan? How do you daydream without a basement or attic?

Where do you disappear after a scolding with floor-to-ceiling windows? Where are the stairs to run up and tumble down?

Gemma had been the one to suggest he model their own salt box. "Familiar, but she's in charge. If she wants to send Daddy to rake up the leaves, she can. Or put Mommy in the basement because she's been mean, she can do that, too. Our house but her house."

Each night, still, he tinkers—glues staircase spindles, finishes a window sash, or papers a wall. Gemma would prefer he demolish it. "It's accusatory," she said. "I can't stand it." So, he covers it with a sheet. Tonight, he'd wired the kitchen circuitry and screwed four tiny bulbs with gossamer filament into a chandelier. When he connected the wires, instead of warming up the empty rooms, instead of offering the promise of furniture and family to come, the light was hard and empty. No one would ever live here.

There is so much Gemma wants to tell Michael. How she isn't asleep. How she never sleeps anymore. Not since their daughter was suctioned and scraped from her as if she wasn't a baby but extraneous matter. Clots. Tissue. As if they didn't already have her name: Annalise. As if they didn't already love her four months, two weeks, and three days too soon.

How she tries to retrospectively tally all the half-glasses of wine she'd had after that first trimester with dinner. And their second anniversary, an unforgivable full glass. Dinner in, instead of out, so she wouldn't get shit from anyone. Michael's first wife had gone through her pregnancies before all the puritanical edicts so he didn't see the harm. Even her midwife had said a swallow every now and then after the first three months was just fine—it might even relax her, which was good, nervous as she was about the pregnancy, about Michael being a father again at fifty-four, about all the things that could go wrong in their attempt to create a life for a child. So: braised short ribs over polenta, spinach sautéed with pancetta, and Cabernet. *I'm not giving up everything for you,* she'd thought. *You can't make me.* Like a bratty thirteen-year-old instead of a thirty-five-year-old mother-to-be.

How she tries to count all the cigarettes she'd smoked in her twenties. Too many. Too many joints, too. And too many other men.

How she's stopped taking Zoloft and Klonopin, squirrels them away in an empty tampon box on the bottom shelf of the linen closet. She dumps them out every morning after Michael leaves for work and counts them, adding the two he'd handed to her the night before and which she'd tucked beneath the mattress. One-and-two-and-three-and-sixty-three-and-seventy. And this very morning, while he was in the basement still working on the dollhouse for nobody's child, she locked herself in the bathroom, sat cross-legged on the tile floor, and stared at the pills lined up in eight neat regiments, one regiment per tile. Handfuls of ten. But there was the movie after lunch. A small thing but enough to keep her here today. She put the pills back in the box.

How she'd bought Michael a Father's Day card in advance, and instead of eating all those pills one bleak afternoon, ate the card instead. Tore the cartoon puppy into bits and pieces and swallowed them.

How she knows her body is a ruin and deliberately so. She doesn't want to live but she isn't sure she wants to die. She is eliminating need. She doesn't need food because that would imply hunger and she doesn't need hunger because she doesn't want to feed this body which she need never love again. Yes, women survive their miscarriages. Her own mother had a miscarriage and within a week was back on the tennis court in her white skirt and ruffled panties thwacking the ball. "You'll get through it," her mother had said in consolation. "In time. We all do."

We all do. What a terrible *we*.

In college, she'd had an abortion with some niggling of conscience—*You could keep it if you wanted to.* But she didn't want to. *It* was *it*: inside then gone. Her boyfriend had driven her to the clinic and she spread her legs, closed her eyes, and went to her British Literature seminar in the afternoon.

It. It. It. That was not that. Now that was this devastation. Did wanting change *it* into *all*? Abortion into miscarriage? How and when do the terms supplant each other? An empty, imprecise word: miscarriage. Miscarriage of justice? This feels unjust. Mis-carried? Tripping on the curb, groceries falling to the ground? Mis-carriage? Horse spooked and the carriage tumbles into a ravine. She certainly missed carrying her, missed her own body's accommodation of her growing daughter, missed the stretching and pulling of muscles and skin and ligaments, missed the accumulating evidence of heartburn and gut rumbles and the flutters.

How her anger at Michael is irrational, but how she can't shake it. Michael, a trust officer at the bank. His job was to predict and manage and protect returns and investments, but he'd never planned for their loss. He was en route to Chicago when the bleeding started, in a meeting when her heart stopped, and by the time he got to the hospital, seven hours later, their daughter was already in a sealed Biohazard waste bucket.

"How dare you," she yelled, when she saw a nurse leaving the operating room with the bucket. "How dare you!"

The nurse squeezed her hand. "I'm sorry," the nurse said, and meant it. "You shouldn't have seen that." A hand on her forehead then, smoothing her hair. A damp washcloth against her cheek.

She didn't want anyone's kindness, only a slap in the face. Just hours earlier, she was stupidly happy spreading butter and blueberry jam on toast, licking her sticky fingers, warming her hands with the green mug of tea. Then the baby moved. Her palm over her belly: *Here. I'm here.* Then quiet. A cooking magazine open on the table and a recipe she would never now cook or eat: quail in green olive and lemon sauce.

A nurse led Michael into the room. Her hand was on her flattened stomach.

"Where have you been?" she said, her voice ugly with rage. She knew, of course: he'd been trying to get here as fast as possible, three hours alone in his car. She could see this in his blotchy face but didn't care.

"I want her back," she said. "Bring her back."

Michael didn't know what she meant.

The nurse said, "They took the remains downstairs to run tests, to find out what went wrong. You'll want to know that for the future."

"I want her back," she said again. "There must be something left."

Something, something, something. Bones in fragments and splinters. That's what she sees now when she closes her eyes at night. And then she tries to put them back together again, tries to imagine her daughter whole and back inside. But there is nothing there: her stomach is a bowl with hipbone handles.

Michael has been uneasy since their visit to the Art Institute last week. Gemma wanted to see the Jasper Johns' "Gray" and he'd wanted to study the miniature rooms. They split up.

Scale: 1: 24. 1:48. 1:144

A portable life? A manageable life? French Salon, English Drawing Room, Connecticut Valley Tavern, California Living Room, and Gothic Church. The exacting details said: *As if.* As if we loved and lost in equal proportion. As if everything we needed was provided—clay baguettes, mohair Jack Russell, matchstick slat crib, paper tulips, plastic stained glass. As if life could be built with tweezers. Neither love nor grief could disrupt the exacting, glued-down candlesticks and flower pots, highboys and wardrobes, pots and pans, books and soap, altars and pews. You were meant to study the craftsmanship and the attention to detail. Scrollwork on the moldings! The microscopic stitches on tapestries! Claw foot legs on the tea table! Look but don't touch. No mess, no collisions.

The Virginia Kitchen, ca. 1778, was untidy: a Windsor chair pushed back from the table, an apple pie on the sideboard, work boots at the bottom of the stairs, a blue, red, and yellow ball in the middle of the room, and beside the table, a child's porcelain doll dressed in pink silk inexplicably left behind. The kitchen door was ajar. Not presence, then, but absence. Life arrested, a house vacant. Who knocked and with what news? Why the rush? Why leave dolly behind? Cholera or scarlet fever? A father dead in the war? A wife seized with cramps? A baby coming too soon or not at all? A bloody bed upstairs or a bloody privy out back? A heart that skipped then stopped?

"Gray." He didn't get it. Gray light bulbs and gray flashlights hanging from gray canvases, gray American flags, gray bullseye targets, gray alphabets. Only "Periscope (Hart Crane)" stopped him. And it wasn't even the painting with its gray circles, nor the explanation for the color streaked through the gray (*color comes undone*), but the fragment of a Hart Crane poem that inspired the painting:

> *...while time clears*
> *Our lenses, lifts a focus, resurrects*
> *A periscope to glimpse what joys or pains*
> *Our eyes can share or answer—then deflects*
> *Us, shunting into a labyrinth submersed*
> *Where each sees only his dim past reversed.*

What was happening to them. The periscope offered a glimpse towards a shared future not sunk in gray despair. The sinking back down into the past, not the dim past but the recent past. The school yard game: *Red Rover, Red Rover. Send our daughter back over.*

Gemma was transfixed by a painting of a wire hanger, or rather, a painting of the shadow of a wire hanger. No, the grayer shadow of the gray shadow of the wire hanger. That is, in front of herself with her back to him, her black overcoat billowing at her sides, shoulder seams drooping down her arms, hands jammed into the pockets. The grayer shadow of the gray shadow of his wife. A crow's shadow against snow.

What did it mean? What was he supposed to see? What did she see? The placard read: *Gray can be considered a material condition. It facilitates the presentation of ideas. It thinks about color through its absence. It avoids the distraction of emotion.*

What was her material condition? Herself. True, but he didn't know what he meant. Herself in the twist of wire? Herself as a despairing repetitive echo?

Gemma turned and smiled.

"I felt you there," she said. "What are you looking at?"

"You," he said. "I'm glad you're here even though you're somewhere else."

She laughed, but she looked angry. "What a strange thing to say." She kissed him quickly on the mouth. "Did you feel that?" she said.

She kissed him again, hard and fast, once, twice, three more times and then turned back to the gray painting again. But then she held up her hand and sawed her thumbnail against her wrist. Blood bloomed in the crescent.

"I feel that," she said. "Which means I'm here."

What else might Gemma tell Michael?

How last week, while running down Crane Road, she stopped at one of those sad trailers: treeless yard, cinderblock steps, mildewed kiddie pool, rusty yellow Tonka truck, muddy lakes. A baby, strapped in a stroller, cheeks wind-blistered, wailed. An orange and brown afghan heaped on the ground. Cold or just lonely? A boy, in man-sized snow boots, whacked a stuffed animal around a puddle with a two-by-four, shouting, "Die, die, die." The baby wailed and pointed at the puddle, at something drowning. A stuffed dog or cat or bear?

She untied her sneaker, retied it, untied it, retied it. Anyone could take a child from here, anyone passing in a car, any pervert. Anyone. And the parents? Where were they? The mother, at least?

"Hey," she said. "Stop that."

The boy dropped the board. "Momma! Momma!"

A momma, then, after all. She ran on, away from the baby, from the idea of what she wanted to do.

How she fell into a muddy ditch this morning, soaking her sneakers and socks, but ran on anyway in the snow because she was running back to the trailer. With each footfall, she whispered, *Less of me. Less of me. Less of me.* What did she mean by this? The chant had changed since the miscarriage. Before, running offered her freedom, a body moving through space and towards the horizon. *Over and out. Over and out. Over and out*, she used to say. Meaning: *across this earth and out of this world.* Consonance—arms pumping, legs cycling, more gallop than jog, like the thoroughbred that raced her along the fence line on Grange Road.

Now, dissonance: off rhythm, stumbling, returning with skinned knees and elbows, gravel pebbling her palms. The earth's axis had shifted, tripping her up. With each footfall, she thought, *She is gone. I am gone. She is gone. I am gone.* She was in exile and found herself doing things she would never have done otherwise.

For instance: stealing. At Value City, she found herself jamming baby clothes into her purse. No—*found herself* is far too passive an admission. Intent is lost. She went to steal. She parked her car close to the entrance in case she had to make a break for it. She was no longer pregnant. No baby due in five months so no need for onesies, snap undershirts, and footed sleepers. No need for the pink dress with smocking across the top and appliquéd roses along the hem, or the white sweater with the pompom drawstring, or the burp cloths, or the stroller blankets. She stole them all anyway. One day she'll be caught. When the security guard hauls her to the back room and forces her to open her purse, will she cry then?

"Please," she might say. "Look. Just inconsequentials."

He will be unmoved.

When Michael arrives, will he tell the guard and manager *Our daughter is dead*? Because she cannot do this. She cannot say this out loud.

They will warn her—*Don't come back*—and shake Michael's hand.

Crazy wife.

For instance: stealing a baby. She ran back to the trailer this morning, casing it, looked through the front window: a television as big as a mattress, two ratty brown recliners, an ashtray full of butts, two beer cans on the coffee table, toys everywhere, and a Chihuahua asleep on a frilly pink pillow.

What was she looking for? Signs of neglect or abuse? Shit in the corner? A belt on the chair? Children abandoned while Mommy went to the bar or to her boyfriend? She wanted self-congratulatory evidence: *my home would be a better home.* But all she could really see was the evidence of a family just scraping by. *As I am*, Gemma thought.

She was still peering through the window when the black Mustang gunned into the front yard and drove all the way up to the front door. She jumped back.

A woman got out of the car, the baby slung against her hip. The mother? Not dressed for the weather—a tee-shirt three-sizes too small, jeans buttoned just at her pubic bone, a tattoo at the waistband, like a bruise, red and purple and black. She was young, younger than Gemma, too young. Maybe the older sister? But there was something in her face—the way it was hardening now as she looked Gemma over—that meant *mother* and *mine* and *mother fucker who are you?*

"You CPS?" the woman said.

Gemma raised her hands in apology.

From inside the car, a dog, an enormous brown dog barked, his face mashed against the windshield, teeth bared. "Shut up, Juno," the woman yelled, though not meaningfully because the dog kept at it. Juno wanted Gemma gone—that was clear.

The older boy was in the front seat crashing his toy truck into the dashboard. No booster seat? Shouldn't he be in one? Wasn't that the law?

And the baby? Not crying. Smiling. And holding on to her sweatshirt with tight fists.

"Your son," Gemma said. "He was playing in the road yesterday when I came running by. There was a truck. Speeding. I thought you should know."

The lie came easily and she waited for the woman's thanks. No.

She was waiting for the woman to offer up her baby—*Take him. You'll take better care of him than I do.*

The woman looked her over—running tights, fleece jacket, her muddy sneakers. Was she too earnest? Too deliberate? Was the longing for *yours to be mine* too evident? She glanced at the boy in the car who was still busy crashing his truck.

"You're not CPS," the woman said. "And if your skinny ass isn't running back to where it came from in two seconds, I let Juno out."

She ran, terrified, slipping in the snow, into the ditch, imagining that dog lunging after her, its paws on her shoulders, its teeth sinking into her neck, imagined giving in. Wouldn't her body in a ditch be easier to bear than her body on a bathroom floor?

How she doesn't say anything at all when Michael runs his hand across her body now, down the length of her spine, resting on her hip.

Their daughter came back in a pail. Michael had removed the lid and cried.

He is awake and Gemma asleep, the dark surrounding them. This is what he thinks about in the middle of the night:

Their daughter came back to them in a pail.

He could tell Gemma nothing was left after all the tests. He could tell her what was left was terrible, unbearable. *Soup*, but he wouldn't say that though it was the truth. But she wouldn't believe that, or if she did, she would want whatever was left.

"Are you okay?" A hand on his shoulder. He'd turned. A young doctor beside him.

"No," he said. No point in lying. "I don't know what to do." He read the nametag: Dr. Gerard Ramashandran, Pediatrics. A doctor he might have met under other circumstances; a doctor who might have held the stethoscope to his daughter's chest, rubbing it first between his fingers to warm it up; a doctor who might have offered his congratulations.

"To do?" the doctor prodded.

"With this," Michael said, and held out the pail. "My daughter."

"I'm not sure I understand what you're telling me," the doctor said. He took his glasses out of his coat pocket and put them on. He looked older then, like someone who would know what to do, and lifted the lid and then his hand covered his mouth. "I see," he said, "I'm sorry. This is a terrible thing."

He frowned. "The hospital takes care of the remains. Whoever gave this to you was thoughtless." His pager went off. He glanced at it.

Michael put the lid back on. He couldn't look at it anymore. "We wanted her back, for burial," he finally said. "But this…." Isn't this what Gemma had meant? She didn't want her to disappear in the incinerator, didn't want her to be a nothing to no one? It's what he meant.

The doctor said, "You want to save something, but not all of this. Is this right?"

Michael nodded. No words for what he wanted.

"I can help," the doctor said. "Will you trust me?" His pager went off again. "I'm sorry," he said. "But we will have to do this quickly." He walked into the kitchenette across the hall, flung open the cabinets, and finally found what he was looking for: a coffee filter. "Here," the doctor said, and held out his hand. "Come."

They walked down the hallway, the doctor's hand on his back, guiding him, helping him along. They went into an operating room. Was this where they'd taken Gemma?

The doctor led him over to a sink and unfolded the filter. "Slowly," the doctor said. "Pour slowly."

Michael was horrified but obeyed. The liquid seeped through the filter. What remained? A nest of bones. Bird bones. A small bird. A hummingbird. Or a handful of shells. Fragments of shells that he could hold in his pocket. His daughter. This was what was left of their daughter.

When he looked up, the doctor was washing his hands. "I am sorry," he said. "But I must get back. I hope this will be enough."

Enough, yes, but never enough.

And now it is Gemma that fits in his pocket. Not enough left to her. He slides out of bed, careful not to disturb his wife. A glass of water, that's all he wants.

• • •

Gemma doesn't say anything when Michael leaves the bed.

This is what she said yesterday on the way home from the doctor's: *Take the back road.*

They'd seen a specialist in high-risk pregnancy, and he was going to help them get pregnant again. They'd waited long enough and it was time to try again. A rational, reasonable, responsible decision.

The back road, the long way home, twice as long in snow, was necessary: enough time and hills and curves to finish the argument they'd started in the doctor's office, enough time to try to be happy again, enough time to try and fail.

She sighed. Michael fiddled, *mindlessly* she thought, with the radio. Christian preaching (God is love!), Christian rock (God is drums, guitars, and swooning crescendos), country (Oh, God, why hast thou forsaken me?), and more happy Christians singing about blessed sons (His son, His son! He died for you!).

"Please," she said.

He switched to the cd: the soprano's voice, delicate, heartbreaking, filled the car. Why should this music irritate, too? Because it was beautiful. She switched it off.

"Do you have to do this?" Michael said. "Just tell me if that's where we're headed now."

Now. What he meant was her silence, the veering off into gray.

"My head just hurts," she said. But she thought, my heart. "I can't get out from under it."

That nurse at the doctor's office, all optimism with her smile and pen and chart, ready to ink in the empty space. "How many children?" she asked.

Gemma was still rearranging the paper sheet across her naked lap, trying to cover her knees. Straightforward enough. Right? Just say a number, the right number. Accuracy counts.

"Pregnancies?"

"One."

"Children?"

The forward march in time from fucking to cell to newborn. It was why they were here, hoping again. Why she was here, imagining again.

"One," she said.

"None," Michael corrected, his way to stop the mess of her explanation.

"One." No way to make one none. One then none.

The nurse hesitated and moved on to her vitals: blood pressure, temperature, pulse.

Am I still alive? she thought. Perfect numbers.

Michael leafed through a parenting magazine, then pointed to a page. "Your niece would love this."

This: Real Live Baby! Press the button? She pees water and poops plastic pellets, giggles and cries, sucks her thumb, slurps on her bottle, and, age-inappropriately says, "Mama, I Love You," in three languages.

"Creepy," she said.

"Wrong," he said. "She'd love it."

The nurse left the room.

She could feel his anger, an anger that was not just a matter of semantics, but full of worry and concern, though these words, worry and concern, were sloppy, inaccurate substitutes for his desperation.

"It's the only way to move forward," the doctor counseled. This was after he'd examined her and told her she was underweight, that if she wanted to get pregnant again, she'd have to eat. "Otherwise," and here, he pointed his finger at her, as if pointing to the tampon box of pills, "otherwise, my dear, you end up dead, too. And what possible good can that do?"

She was glad Michael wasn't in the room for this, that she'd told him to leave for the exam.

So, the long drive home through tunnels of snow, the road slick and bumpy with ice, the gray sky darkening, the lid closing on them.

"If you don't want to try again, just tell me," Michael said. "But I thought it was what we wanted."

"Want. I don't know what I want except, of course, what I can't want," she said.

"I want you back," he says. "You're a ghost."

"What you want, what everybody wants is to fuck with grief's chemistry. Zoloft, Wellbutrin, Lexapro. Line up the bottles. Feel better. I'm not ready for better. Sure. I'll smile for you. I'll say, 'No child. I have no child.' But I don't believe it."

At the side of the road, crows were pecking a dead deer. They scattered into the pines as they drove by.

"Fucking birds," she said. "Fucking winter." Roads spattered with blood and guts and fur. The running tab for the drive back? Deer, deer, deer, raccoon, deer, groundhog, deer. And all the crows pecking into the bodies.

His hand moved to her back, a still hand, a pause for patience and kindness.

When they climbed into bed that night, she'd offered her body in consolation, coaching herself through it: Put hand on back. Kiss neck. Look away, at the wall, the ceiling, at anything else but him. Raise hips. Hold tight. A little longer. Now let go.

Michael let go first. "Look at me," he said. "No pity fucks. When you're ready, let me know."

What she wants is for Michael to throw her from the bed to the floor, to yank her nightgown to her hips and fuck, to hurt her. What she wants, Dear Doctor, is to die. Just until she is steady again.

The trash can is on its side and he is on his hands and knees on the tile floor, dissecting the garbage under the spotlights, sorting it across three plastic bags when Gemma walks into the kitchen, groggy, barefoot, and pink-robed.

She rubs at her eyes. "What kind of archaeology are you doing?"

"Not food," he says, pointing to the first pile. Greasy paper towels, shredded junk mail, three toilet paper tubes, a light bulb.

He points to the second. "My food." Toast rinds, orange peel, oatmeal scrapings, Snickers wrapper, three of four beer bottle caps, lamb chop bones from the previous night's dinner.

Then the third. "Your food." One bottle cap, sandwich wadded inside a napkin, the other half of her half of the salmon also inside a napkin, two intact lamb chops, coffee grinds, empty Tylenol bottle, gum wrappers.

She tightens her robe, knotting the belt until she can't breathe. "And you lost what? Your cellphone? Wedding ring?"

"You. Do you eat anything at all, Gemma? Because it's all here."

She reaches down, picks up the sandwich, takes an enormous bite, and swallows it down whole. "There. Eat. Ate. Has been eaten."

"Please," he says, but doesn't know what he's asking.

She turns and spits the food into the sink. "I can't do this," she says.

He wraps his arms around her and she gives way, falling against him. How easily she fits inside them. How easily she might break. He is not sure what she means by *this* but he can't do it anymore either. What he thinks about is not his dead daughter but another portrait inside another locket. A woman on a bed, eyes closed, hands folded at her chest. Her long brown hair a waterfall across her shoulders. A white gown and veil. *Sarah Mackie, The Dead Bride, 1819-1843.* Open shut open shut. The husband must have pinned her to his heart.

• • •

The basement is dark, the dollhouse shrouded.

Gemma thinks: ghost house ghost house ghost house.

Michael thinks: This. This is all I know to do.

He removes the sheet, tosses it to the ground.

"Watch," he says, and reaches into the attic. Nothing else to show for his time but this. He connects the wires to the voltage box, then flips the switch. The house lights come up.

Gemma reaches into a room—the kitchen? the parlor? the dining room? without furniture impossible to know—and runs a fingertip over the tiny bulb.

"I wish I could live in it," she says. "I wish I could swallow the light."

What they know:

They will go back to bed. She may sleep or not. He will not rest easy or will. In the early morning, they will still be here and it will still be dark and there will still be snow. They will turn on the lights and drink their coffee together. And he will make breakfast. Pancakes and warm maple syrup. Bacon and sausage. Sugared grapefruit. They will sit at the table and bless the food. She will try again to eat.

The Assassin of Bucharest

Powell sat on a bench beneath a linden at Cişmigiu Park watching an old man having a sponge bath in the artificial lake. Bucharest. How clean could the water be? The water from the faucets in his rental apartment ran orange. The old man had stripped to his underwear, doused himself with water, and was scrubbing his calves, thighs, elbows, and chest with the yellow sponge, wringing it over the top of his head. He was oblivious to the happy couples rowing past in boats rented by the hour, oblivious to the black swans honking at his encroachment, oblivious to the teenagers giggling in derision.

A certain freedom to his craziness, though Powell didn't think the man was crazy. Despite the public bath, he had brought a sponge and a towel, and folded his gray pants and blue sweater in a neat stack beside a tree. Forethought and afterthought.

If it wasn't for Powell's son, Henry, pushing his Matchbox cars on the pavement, he might have crashed into the lake himself, though the Poliția would not likely treat a foreign bather the same as a native, and that would lose him his Fulbright. He could always explain that he was seeking an aquatic perspective on the magnolia that fringed the lake.

But he would never leave his son, not in that way, not even for a momentary reprieve. Henry's mother, Powell's wife Beth, had left—though he had understood it wasn't truly her choice. "I'm ruining our good," she wrote. He was teaching Dickinson to bored freshmen and Henry was in kindergarten making a paper maché dragon mask when his wife pulled onto an off-road in the San Gabriels and swallowed four bottles of stockpiled Lithium. He only knew something was wrong, beyond the normal day-to-day wrongs that he was used to with Beth, when his son's teacher called: *Thirty minutes past pick-up. Did something happen?*

Did something happen? A question replayed as a statement of fact.

He looked at Henry, at his brown hair, shaggy, curling at the nape of his neck, and the smear of ketchup across his striped shirt. Henry had woken up that morning feeling homesick, so Powell took him to McDonald's. Henry sat cross-legged on the pavement, shoving his cars into the grass in some imagined high speed crash. He was lonely—no friends but his father and Ileana, his babysitter and Powell's Romanian student. The students at the Cambridge International School were well-to-do and rather stuck-up; while they spoke English as required during school, they refused to speak English to Henry. Powell's rationalization: better lonely in Romania than in despair in LA. A deliberate dislocation to break their grief.

Six months earlier, while driving to the store for frozen pizza and frozen potstickers and rocky road ice cream, their usual Friday night dinner, Powell had told Henry about the move. His son was strapped in his car seat, so the conversation would be easier than if they were home.

"An adventure. Just you and me." He smiled at Henry in the rearview mirror. Romania was not his first choice but it was the only opening, and they needed to be somewhere else.

Henry was battling an alien on his Nintendo. "That's not fun."

"Dracula lived there. We can go to his castle."

Henry's eyes met his in the mirror. "Do we have to kill vampires?"

"Stake through the heart, but they're all gone."

"Gone like Mom?"

Now, Henry had abandoned his Matchbox cars and stood at the lake's edge staring at the old man who was smiling at him, gesturing with his hand as if encouraging his son to wade in.

"Bună Ziua," Henry said.

"Henry!" Powell shouted. "Time to go home." He didn't believe his son would jump in, but Powell was vigilant.

Ileana, Henry's babysitter, was also Powell's student in his "Great American Poets" course at the university, his attempt to introduce the Romanian students to marquee stars: Whitman, Dickinson, Frost, Stevens, Lowell, Plath. Ileana raised her hand and said, "Whitman says, 'I lean and loafe in grass.' Dangerous. Under Ceauşescu, illegal to step on grass in parks."

After class, she stood beside his desk. "Scuze," she said. She was nervous and tucked her brown hair behind her ear but it fell forward into her face. Her face was angular, sharp, and even her speech was clipped though that might have been her accent. "See?" she said, and held out her phone, scrolling down the screen. "Text poems." The texts were in Romanian so impossible to read: interesting or banal? Then she leaned into the desk and looked at him in hard assessment. "I know what you need."

Boundaries were fluid here. Students expected him to have coffee with them after class and the women suggested drinks at night clubs. Some students were "officially" on his roster but actually attending Swedish or German universities. His colleagues smoked in their offices, drank at lunch time, and fucked their students. In their estimation, he was an amusing American prig. In his? Enduring his wife's absence.

Ileana tapped the desk with her phone and said, "At welcome party, I see your son. Yes? Maybe you need nanny. I do this."

On the walk home from Cişmigiu, Henry counted dogs. Stray dogs. One: curled up under the back tire of a silver Mercedes. Two: in the doorway of a dilapidated, Art Nouveau apartment building. Three: sleeping in a cardboard box. Four: sitting on a bus bench. Five: inside a derelict phone booth. Six: nursing puppies under a shrub. Seven: skulking down a cobblestone alley with its tail tucked. Eight: lying in the middle of the side-walk, pedestrians stepping around and over it. Nine: waiting at their building for Henry to give him a treat, any treat, this time half of his hot pretzel that Powell had bought at the bakery at the top of their block. All day long, a fat man in a flour-dusted apron looped dough into knots and pretzels onto a conveyor belt that moved through a wood-burning oven.

Powell and Henry lived at Piața Lahovari above the Sex Shop. Henry was interested in the window display—enormous dildos he mistook for toys.

Dog Nine lived in the Sex Shop's doorway which smelled of piss, human not dog. Its long, matted fur was tangled with leaves and bits of paper. It barked at the neighborhood junkies, but when they approached, the dog wagged its tail.

"Bun câine!" Henry said to the dog and held the pretzel out to it.

"Not so close," Powell said.

Henry tossed the pretzel to the ground.

"The dog might have worms or rabies. You need to keep your distance."

"Why can't we take him with us?" Henry said.

In another life, in another place, back home for instance, seeing this dog with its plaintive face, he might have said, "Let's take him home and give him a bath." But this was not their home, not even their apartment, and they'd be gone in eight weeks. Who knew where the dog came from or where it went at the end of the day? Maybe it would take the pretzel from his son's hand, but maybe it would lunge, bite, draw blood, refuse to let go. *That's how it happens*, he wanted to say. *That's how you die*. But he didn't.

"The dog belongs here. He helps Serghei."

As if on cue, Serghei came out of the Sex Shop with a bag of chocolate cookies and a bottle of beer, his cheap leather jacket zipped to his neck to contain his formidable stomach. He tossed Dog Nine a cookie and lit a cigarette.

"Bună Ziua," Serghei said, and handed Henry the cookies. "I have beer," he said. "You and tată are skinny like dog. You need mamă to cook. That is what mamă do for her baby."

Henry was quiet for the elevator ride to the sixth floor and all the way through dinner. At bedtime, he turned away from Powell's kiss.

When Henry was a baby, he couldn't, wouldn't, sleep. Beth sat in the rocking chair, nursing him for hours on end. She was loopy, wide-eyed, desperate for sleep. "Please," she whispered, "do something." He walked with Henry around the house, set him in the car seat on the washing machine, put him next to the stereo speakers. One night, he packed his son in the car and drove twenty miles down the 101 and back. Henry grew quiet and fell asleep.

A few months earlier, they drove that route again: Henry had been seized by night terrors, waking up and screaming for his mother. After a few sleepless nights, Powell buckled his son in the car and started the engine. Henry quieted but stayed awake, staring out the window at the empty road. He asked the questions on the return: "Did Mom hurt when she died? Couldn't we help her?"

No. No? Probably not? Maybe not? Her psychiatrist, in an unorthodox debriefing, told Powell that Beth was determined—just consider the method—and Powell had done everything he could. He loved his wife, and she loved him, but her illness had no regard for love.

His students were reading Dickinson—her poems were enigmatic, like their fragmented texts.

He asked Ileana to read, and she did so with halting vehemence.

"The Brain has Corridors—surpassing/Material Place. Ourself behind ourself concealed—/Should startle most—Assassin hid in our Apartment." She stopped, shifted forward in her seat, and continued, "He bolts the Door—/O'erlooing a superior spectre—/Or More—." She sighed. The tangled words were tiring.

"Imagine Dickinson in her room, staring out her window into the yard, into the trees, maybe into the sky—feeling what?" he asked.

The students started to put away their books, anxious for him to finish. But he wasn't done. "Think about that house. Think about her polite stanzas and the danger inside them," he said. "We are our own assassins."

• • •

That morning, his wife had driven Henry to school. The only thing out of the ordinary, and in retrospect, entirely significant. Usually, she had difficulty in the mornings because of her medications which made her sleepy, made her irritable, and since he needed to be on campus early, he usually dropped Henry at school. She was the one who got Henry dressed and fed and out the door with a kiss.

But that morning? She was up early, dressed, and said she wanted to take Henry to school, be a proper mom, take advantage of feeling good. Powell worried—she smiled too brightly, sang, "Do-Re-Mi" as she rushed around the kitchen, and swept Henry off his feet—but he didn't want to break the spell.

"I'm trying, Powell," she said, then got into the car with Henry and drove off.

Later, Henry's teacher would tell him that his wife was crying at the classroom door. "I didn't know," the teacher said.

But Powell stopped her. "She didn't know herself. Not all of it."

The assassin in wait. When did she count the pills? Before dressing Henry in his blue jeans and Star Wars shirt? After pouring his bowl of Lucky Charms and glass of orange juice? Or the night before, after dinner, after kissing him to sleep?

He sold her car without ever opening its doors again, only looking through the car's windows to imagine his wife curled up on the back seat. Professionals scrubbed it clean. He drove out Route 2 to mile marker 451, to the stand of firs. Why here? Had she scouted the location or simply driven forward, stopping when she felt she'd gone far enough?

• • •

"Your son is not happy," Ileana said. She sipped her coffee. "I take him to playground. He run and play, but I don't think he have fun."

They were having coffee in a café, talking about Ileana's essay on Dickinson, but now they had come around to his son.

Powell glanced out the window. On the corner, a Roma woman with an infant strapped to her back, holding open a box of trinkets: plastic watches and tiny toys for a few lei each. A young boy, holding his own box, ran up to her and handed over a fistful of money, then sprinted back across the busy avenue. Powell thought of Henry at school, hunched over his desk with his pencil, tracing h-o-u-s-e, wondering when they would be going h-o-m-e, or maybe he was standing alone in the schoolyard, watching the other children play and wondering how they could laugh.

"Henry likes you," Powell said. "He watches out the window to see when you're coming."

Ileana ran her finger around the rim of her coffee cup as if in divination. "Nice for me, yes? But I know him for a short time and I think he is not waiting for me."

He would like to tell her about Henry waiting for his mother after school. The teacher told Powell that his son had stood in the doorway, bundled in his red coat, holding his Star Wars lunchbox and his drawing of a green dinosaur eating yellow chickens and an announcement of parent-teacher conferences. She told him to sit at the table while she called his mom. *Maybe she was stuck in traffic*, she said. But he stood in the doorway for an hour until Powell arrived.

Powell smiled at Ileana. "It's you. You save him from me."

The Roma boy ran back across the street to the woman—his mother?—and he showed her his box, pointing at it. She yelled at him, though Powell couldn't hear her through the glass. The boy shook his head, yelled back, and then the woman raised her hand, slapped him across the face, knocking him and the box of toys to the ground, and then she kicked him in his side. The boy gathered the toys back in the box and walked down the street. He didn't look back. His small victory? Parents leave their marks. So much necessary repair.

The Bucharest Natural History Museum was a throwback to Communist-era misinformation. A diorama featured plastic busts in a "progression of cultures": from a black monkey head to a Samoan head complete with voluptuous breasts, to an enormous blond, blue-eyed "Nord European" head. The dinosaur exhibit had a few splindly skeletons that were more suggestive of horses than velociraptors, but most were plastic toys arranged inside glass display cases. Toybox approximation.

"A volcano!" Henry ran over to the display, a large-scale plaster and paint model such as a sixth-grader might slop together for the science fair.

"Not very dangerous," Henry said.

"We're at a safe distance, but do you know how hot that is in real life?"

Henry shrugged. "As hot as the sun?"

"Hot enough to burn you up. Like how the wood turns to ash in the fireplace?"

Henry leaned over the railing and stuck his finger in the red lava. "I didn't," he said, "and I got close."

"That's not real," Powell said and ruffled his son's long hair. Henry needed a haircut. But where in Bucharest? No Kiddie Cuts here.

Henry shoved his hand into the volcano as if grabbing for fire.

"Don't," Powell said. "There's a railing."

"This is a dumb volcano," he said. "Nothing here is real."

Powell strolled through Herăstrău Park intent on a bench in the sun. A stack of essays to grade on Frost's, "Desert Places."

The park was landscaped with discordant statues that stood in schmaltzy though poignant homage to civilization: caryatids, Venus, Prometheus, Hercules, Leonardo da Vinci, Shakespeare, Chopin, Beethoven, Chekhov, Twain, Darwin, Goethe and most absurd, the Alley of the Heads—enormous bronze heads of the European Union founding members. He leaned into a colossal ear.

"Hello, Konrad Adenauer," he said, then recited Frost: "I have it in me so much nearer home—To scare myself with my own desert places." He leaned further, the metal against his lips. "Beth," he said as if her ghost were inside listening for him. He almost never said her name, not aloud anyway, because who would answer?

A child shouted into another ear. And a woman on tip-toe giggled as she spoke. What were they saying? "I have a cat!" or "I'm in love!" What would Henry say into an ear willing to hear everything and give nothing away?

Dog Nine sat in the Sex Shop doorway at good-natured attention. Powell reached down to pat the dog's head. Its tail thumped against the concrete. He could see why Henry wanted to bring the dog home. Dog Nine was steadfast, attached to this corner of the city, grateful for crumbs and a few kind words.

He pulled out his ham-and-cheese sandwich from his satchel. When did the dog eat something other than Serghei's chips and cookies? He tossed half of the sandwich on the ground. The dog sniffed at it, then wolfed it down. The dog looked at him, at the other half of the sandwich in his hand. Powell patted him again on the head, imagining the dog curled up at one end of the apartment's ugly green couch. The dog might sigh, stretch, circle for a new spot, and then sleep. How difficult could it be to bring the dog back to the States? Vaccination papers?

He offered the dog the rest of the sandwich. A quick sniff, then the dog lunged, and its teeth clamped down on Powell's hand.

"Fuck!" He kicked the dog in its side.

Dog Nine yelped and ran off.

He inspected his fingers. No broken skin. So fine, but he knew better. It was why he wouldn't let Henry get close to the dogs.

Powell sat on a bench at the edge of the crowded playground. Mothers were gathered on the perimeter, smoking, gossiping, and calling to their children every few minutes to make sure they hadn't wandered beyond the park's gates. "Cosmina! Mihai! Petru!" One woman held out a brown, grease-stained paper bag. Her daughter ran over and pulled out a square of strudel, apple plăcinta; her tiny fingers were dusted in confectioner's sugar.

Henry was on the swing, pumping his legs back and forth, and as Powell watched his son, he wondered if things were precipitously worse, if coming to Bucharest had been a selfish maneuver, and it was now time to pack it in. But really, he worried about whether Henry, like him, was turning to an inside Beth instead of the outside world. *Come back as you are*, he said into the ear.

On the upswing, Henry straightened his legs, gliding through the air, eyes closed. Did he imagine himself a dolphin, an airplane, a spaceship? They'd all kept too much to themselves.

Henry pumped harder and higher, then let go, flying through the air, and before hitting the ground, his face opened in easy, unequivocal joy.

Powell ran over, but Henry shrugged him off.

"The best ever," Henry said.

"Do you hurt anywhere?" Powell said.

Henry turned his hands over. Tiny pebbles pressed into his palms, a knuckle scraped and bleeding. "Nothing hurts."

"Maybe not now but it will," Powell said. He kissed the knuckle—his son's blood in his mouth, copper on his tongue, the same blood that passed through Henry's heart.

When they left the apartment for their walk to the park, Dog Nine was curled under the Sex Shop's overhang. Rain earlier, so its fur was wet and smelled of neglect. Sunday, so the Sex Shop was closed. No cookies or chips. The dog lifted its head, thumped its tail. All was forgiven. Powell pulled out a wadded napkin from his jacket pocket and put it on the ground. Six leftover meatballs. The dog ate them all in one bite.

"What if he wasn't here?" Henry asked. "And you had to carry meatballs all day?"

"He's always here," Powell said. "And if not, we'd find another hungry dog."

Herăstrău Park and the Alley of the Heads were empty, just a few determined stragglers walking through the gray drizzle to somewhere else.

"I tell her whatever I want," Powell said.

"She won't get mad?"

"Anything. Choose any ear."

Henry ran over to a head and leaned into the metal ear, his red raincoat wrapped around him like a signal flare. Was he summoning his mother? Henry would wait forever. Time to walk back, stop at a café for coffee and hot chocolate, buy pretzels from the fat baker, an extra for the dog. Powell needed to tell Henry that though they were diminished, they were enough.

Home Burial

They were holding out for the dog. Even Jonathan, their son, gave his tacit approval for a divorce before he left for college. "Really," he'd said, "it's obvious."

Moriah looked at Ben in astonishment. Was it *so* obvious? She thought they'd done a good job hiding the tenacious decline of their marriage. After all, over the past two years, they'd mostly seen Jonathan at breakfast and dinner, while bumping around each other's coffee mugs and passing the steak and potatoes, or cheering him on from the bleachers at his lacrosse games in his team colors, or on the occasional weekend night when he wasn't out with friends, while watching zombies get slayed on their enormous television. She and Ben tried to keep a united front despite the toll his brief affair had exacted, and to be fair, she had pulled away from him before that, though this wasn't an excuse. However, they were both in agreement: Jonathan mattered most. See him to college and then decide where things stood. But Daisy, their dog, got sick, a malingering cancer, and their ending was on hold.

She watched her husband from the bay window in the kitchen, her hands pressed against the cold glass. Ben stood between the dormant hydrangea bush with its desiccated blossoms and the towering, denuded elm, staring at the ground with a shovel in his hands. He cleared a swath of leaves and started digging, anchoring the shovel with his foot, then chucking dirt to the side.

Daisy snored on the dog bed on the floor. Her once compact, muscular body was now gaunt and her gleaming sandy fur dull and patchy.

"C'mon Daisy," she said, "Let's see what's going on."

The dog had difficulty standing; her hind legs splayed out behind her. Moriah gathered them together to help her up. Still no guarantee she'd make it outside. The inoperable tumor had made it almost impossible to walk. The vet had recommended putting her down. Tomorrow. That was what they'd decided.

Daisy hobbled a few feet into the grass and collapsed again. She lay down on her side and rolled in the grass, panting at the effort and pleasure.

Moriah bent over and scratched her belly. "There, there. Good girl."

The dog thumped her tail. Such easy happiness. Meanwhile, Ben was digging his hole to China.

"What's it for?" she called out.

He had a rhythm going now and the pile of dirt had grown larger, the hole big enough to plant a skyscraper.

"Can't say," he said, his voice strained.

"Can't say? Or don't know?" She thought he might be doing one of those things men do when they channel their feelings into action. Daisy was about to die. No. They were her benevolent executioners. So rather than talk about it or sit beside Daisy and stroke that sweet spot behind her ear, he was going to exhaust himself by chucking dirt, pounding through igneous and sedimentary rocks until he got to that molten volcanic core.

Ben leaned against his shovel, looked at their dog, and smiled, suddenly younger, more like the man who could stop her heart. When they first met, she'd been a paralegal for an overbearing tax attorney, yawning her way through the work. She'd bolt out the door on her lunch hour for the city streets, pacing up and down Broadway trying to wake herself up, remind herself that she was twenty-two and alive and in her body. Then she met Ben, and he looked at her with such intensity that she knew she wouldn't die in a stale, fluorescent-lit conference room looking for barely-legal loopholes for corporate tax returns, but would live with this man in some brighter life.

"I don't want to say," Ben said. "Not out loud."

She ruffled her hand through the fur along Daisy's spine, feeling the hard knobs of bone. Impossible to believe their girl would be gone, though old lady at thirteen. Still the difficulty of reconciling herself to this, even if it was the humane thing to do, which it was.

"Are you kidding?" she said and leaned into the dog. "We've already decided how it's going to be."

Ben was already crossing the yard, already running his hand down Daisy's wide head and across the long plane of her body. Moriah could see this was no easy matter, this first goodbye.

"Cremation," she said. "The vet will send her out."

"No," he said. "She's ours. We're keeping her with us."

She looked at the hole. What would happen if they divorced and sold the house? Should she even bring this up? The new owners' kids would be run back and forth across Daisy?

"The Neighborhood Association has rules," she said. Rules for everything: only approved trees and shrubs, a twenty-day window for holiday decorations, and immediate removal of all dead and diseased plants. A pet cemetery wouldn't be up to code.

"Fuck them," Ben said. "She stays here."

They weren't dog people, not at the start. Traveling people. Vietnam, Zanzibar, Mongolia. A wall of pictures: Ben on a bicycle in front of a stone temple, a monkey climbing on the back wheel; Moriah inside an open, arched window, the gold dome of a mosque in the distance; both on horseback in the Gobi Desert, their guide, Batbayar, grinning his toothless smile. After Jonathan, their travels were less exotic but even their son had a full passport—Greece, Italy, Spain, Argentina, Costa Rica. They believed that travel, an immersion in the world, in a world of difference, expanded the boundaries of their lives. Their suburban brick colonial set back in the cul-de-sac of the conservative neighborhood on the commuter line wasn't as suffocating when they could take flight twice a year.

Daisy changed all that. Boarding kennels wouldn't take a pit bull. Even when Moriah called her a "*Bull Terrier.*"

"Sorry," they said. "Liability. Nothing against your dog, but dogs like yours are the problem."

Occasionally, a dog sitter was willing to watch Daisy for a short weekend, but who could do Laos in three days? So, they rented houses in Hilton Head and Cape Cod, pet-friendly places, lying to the owners. "A mutt," she'd say. "A shelter dog." Not exactly a lie because they didn't know Daisy's exact breed and, in fact, wasn't she a sheltered dog, a gift from one of Ben's big clients? Drug trafficking. Acquittal. Ben went to his client's house with papers for him to sign and found him in the backyard with three big dogs, four pups.

"Family," the man said. "This is it. Me and my dogs."

Ben expected the dogs to lunge and snarl and leap for his neck in one big happy dog-fighting pack. But his client was an Alpha with a gun, and the minute one of the dogs got too close to Ben or started growling, the man jammed the dog to the ground by the scruff of its neck. Ben left with a puppy. No way to say "No," not to that kind of gratitude.

A name? Counter the threat of a pit bull with sunny, bouncy *Daisy*.

Moriah was chopping carrots for the roasting pan. Slices rolled off the cutting board to the floor. Daisy would have never missed out on floor scraps—potato skins, ice cubes, pencil shavings, bottle caps; everything sampled and then vomited back in the middle of the night on the bedroom floor. But now, she stayed on her bed, indifferent, her breathing labored.

Daisy was thirteen. Not ancient in real time, but in human years, about ninety-one, a senior citizen, an unsteady creature when she walked, unable to climb stairs, eyes cloudy with cataracts, incontinent from the cancer, but steady, still, in her knowledge of them, in who they were, still thumping her tail at Ben and Moriah, still licking their hands and feet. They were her pack. She hadn't turned on them in her pain or forgetting.

Moriah? If she was a dog? Three-hundred-and-forty-three human years old. An old hag—toothless, mangy, and gassy, with nails dragging on the hardwoods. And why she'd been thrown over for a younger woman. In the reverse, in dog years, she was a spritely seven-year-old, capable of catching a Frisbee fifty yards out and instantly ferocious when threatened—teeth bared, hackles raised, tail pointed, nothing soft and forgiving, nothing that would allow another bitch in her yard.

She put the carrots in the pan with the celery, onions, potatoes and chicken, and drizzled olive oil on top. For whom was this feast? Two breasts would suffice, but an entire roast chicken with trimmings? A funeral supper. An impulsive decision. With Jonathan gone, she rarely made the effort. She and Ben fended for themselves like hapless adolescents: sandwiches, cereal, take-out, take-out leftovers. When she did cook? Spaghetti with jarred sauce or a Cobb salad. Nothing for Daisy to sit up and take notice of.

Ben walked through the back door and stood at the sink washing his hands. How could he be so calm? She wanted to tell him to move the dishes, to wash in the basement utility sink, that this was the dirt from Daisy's grave. But what she was angry about was how he was staring out the window like this wasn't anything at all. Like he hadn't just dug their dog's grave but transplanted a forsythia bush.

"I called Jonathan," she said, suddenly.

Ben wiped his hands on a towel. "I thought we agreed. Wait until after his exam tomorrow."

"We did. But I don't. Daisy is his dog, too. Daisy slept in his bed every night."

Ben squatted beside the dog, his hand on her head. "It's easier for us. But Jonathan? He's alone in his dorm room. Yeah, I know, life goes on, and she's a dog, but she's not. She's us."

Daisy wasn't always easy going. Fights at the dog park. Growling at strangers. Maybe it *was* the breed. For a time, a shock collar and a crate. When people came to the house, she was locked in their bedroom where she savaged chew toys.

"Really," Moriah insisted, "she's sweet. She sleeps with Ben every night, curled at his feet. She just doesn't trust anyone outside the family." But she could see that most people didn't believe her. Strike one, two, and three: Daisy was a pit bull.

They had to pay extra in homeowner's insurance because of this fact.

There had been difficulties with the next-door neighbor when it was clear that Daisy was not going to grow up to be a Golden Retriever. The neighbor was concerned about *his children's safety as well as the value of his home.* The neighbor called Daisy a *pimp ghetto dog,* as if he wasn't just a dorky mortgage broker from the suburbs who watched *Law & Order.* But he was persistent and took his case to the Neighborhood Association.

"Look at this," Ben said, waving the piece of paper at Moriah. "A summons to appear before the High Court of Our Peers."

Jonathan was on the ground rolling a ball across the room for Daisy. Each time she brought it back to him, he reached into her mouth for the slimed-up ball.

They won their case though understanding that their neighbor would never give Daisy a break, never wave hello on an evening walk, never come over for a barbecue with Daisy tethered in the yard (and would never be invited over). When Jonathan's friends came to the house, it was easier to sequester Daisy rather than reassure parents about her temperament and training, because once the parents saw Daisy, their kids were unavailable to come back to the house.

At one point, they faltered. Daisy was only eight months old. Their love for her more benevolent than immutable since they'd only had her for four months.

"Jonathan will hardly remember her," Moriah had said. "We could get a different dog. Not right away."

"Not my choice if I could choose again," Ben said.

"You had a choice," she said. "You always do. You were just…." She didn't say 'afraid,' because she didn't like to think of her husband as someone afraid of his clients, of anyone. She would have been afraid in that backyard surrounded by razor-wire and pit bulls. But it was more than fear, wasn't it? Ben saw those dogs, their bodies marred with cuts and scars, missing eyes and ears, and thought he could save one.

To be honest, wasn't she afraid? Wasn't Daisy really part of their pack? If they kept her, she would live for at least twelve more years which meant twelve years of their neighbors' ire, of skulking on walks, of apologizing for their dog, of always being on alert to their dog's misbehavior that might turn into malign behavior.

She went to the animal shelter. Would they take Daisy? They showed her the dogs up for adoption. Two long rows. Cage after cage, dog after dog, variations, most of them, of pit bulls huddled in the back corners of the cages, tails between their legs or barking and lunging at the bars. She knelt beside a cage, coaxing a dog with a biscuit. It took two cautious steps, eyed her warily, then ran back, hunched and trembling in the corner, refusing to meet her eyes.

She left and knew that Daisy was theirs.

Ben stood at the counter dicing chicken and potatoes for Daisy. He set it on a plate on the floor beside her.

"Last supper," Moriah said, putting the leftovers into containers. "How is that possible?"

Ben slid the dish closer to Daisy. "C'mon girl," he said. "Your favorite."

"What are we going to do?" she said. She meant tomorrow, after Daisy, but also the tomorrow after that.

"We'll know when it's time," he said, echoing what the vet said to them all those months ago when he told them about the tumors.

They sat at the table waiting for Daisy to eat, but she was tired and in pain. They sat cross-legged on the floor beside her and stroked her and told her how lucky they were to have had her as their dog.

• • •

Moriah stood in the door of her son's room looking at what he'd left behind in his college exodus. Trophies and books. His guitar. Star Wars figures. No choice loving him. No, of course there was choice in love, wasn't there? They had chosen to love Daisy—difficult to love, a dog no one else loved. And Ben. After falling in love, wasn't staying in love a choice, requiring active effort? She'd faltered somewhere along the way in the busyness of raising a child and working. In married love, they'd failed, had given up.

Where did he find the time or the energy for an affair? Maybe, for him, it resurrected their own early years, how she'd rescued him from the tedium of the conference room. Ben had come to her, repentant. A short-lived mistake. Another attorney. Moriah never asked who the woman was, never wanted a name to fill in the space.

When she'd finished shouting, when the anger quieted, she understood his affair as symptomatic of the space already between them. They liked each other, sat at the table and broke bread. But would they choose each other again? Would they choose to fall in love again? And now there was tomorrow and the terrible choice that love required. Could they stand together as the vet slipped in the syringe? As Daisy took a last breath? Would they look away or hold steady?

They were trying to carry Daisy upstairs.

"I'll get my hands under her butt, then you get your hands under her shoulders," Ben said. "On three."

Since Daisy could no longer climb the stairs and was incontinent, she'd been sleeping in the kitchen for three months. Unacceptable on her last night. They eased her onto their bed, onto the plastic shower curtain.

"There you go, girl," Moriah said. She faced the wall to undress.

"You do that," Ben said, "and it's like we're strangers."

"Aren't we, mostly?"

She climbed into bed and faced him. "Help me pull her up between us. Remember the first night? How she trembled and whimpered? She was so scared of us? And the only thing that helped was pulling her up here between us?" She put her hand on Daisy's head.

Ben touched her arm. The small weight was startling but she didn't shrug him off.

"We've been a good pack," he said. "The four of us."

She thought of Jonathan's empty room, his bed now always made. "He won't ever really come back. Just two of us."

"Sweet girl," he said to Daisy who was already asleep. "Not yet." He tapped her paw. He looked at Moriah. "I wanted her to stay awake. Idiotic, right? Of course, she's going to sleep. Just another night. She doesn't know."

"But that's it. She's with us and it's just another night of sleep," she said. "Remember from obedience class? She takes her cues from us."

Daisy was lying on the exam table, a patch of fur shaved by the technician from her front leg. "That's a good girl," Ben said. She thumped her tail.

Moriah ran her hand across Daisy's head. How many times had she wished for an easier dog? "You are so good," she said. "You are so loved." She kissed Daisy between the eyes, breathing her in.

And then the vet was in the room.

"Hello, folks," he said. "I'm sorry for this, but we know it's the right time." He held Daisy's leg in one hand, a syringe in the other. "First, I'm going to inject a relaxant so she stays calm, then the euthanizing agent."

Moriah bit her lip and tasted blood. Ben's hands were across Daisy's body, rising and falling with her breath.

"Wait," she said and walked around the table so she could face her dog, so she could hold Daisy's gaze in her own. She didn't want her dog to be alone in her dying.

"Okay," she said, and then reached for Ben's hand.

Even wrapped up in a sheet, they were having trouble maneuvering Daisy out of the trunk. They stumbled up the driveway, around the side of the house, and to the backyard.

"Dead weight," Ben said, meaning to be funny, meaning to be not funny, meaning to ease their way. He clasped Daisy's hind legs through the sheet with one hand, the other under her rump.

Moriah laughed. "Wouldn't the asshole love to see us now?" That had been the neighbor's name between them for years.

Her hands supported Daisy's neck and shoulders. She was walking backwards and just wanted to get to the grave without dropping her because Daisy wouldn't shake it off and run after her ball or a squirrel. No choice, just dead. "Please, please, please, please," she whispered while staggering across the grass, "let us get there."

And then they were there and lowered her to the grass.

"Hold on," Ben said. He disappeared inside the house.

She knelt beside Daisy, her hand feeling for the body beneath the sheet. Ben was right. Better here. Her yard.

Ben returned with her bed and toys, and dropped them to the bottom of the hole, pushing the bed with his foot until it covered the dirt. They took up their ends of Daisy and lowered her into the grave. They stared down at the white heap that was still their dog.

"You were always the dog for us," Moriah said. She watched Ben shovel the dirt back into the grave. He was no longer young. Tired and sad now, like a man without his dog, a father without his son, a husband without his wife. But he was beautiful, too, working in the afternoon's ending sunshine, even at this grim task. How could this—standing over this grave—be their end?

Ben smoothed the dirt over the mound and then planted a gardening stake and hung her collar from the curved end. He jangled the tags with his finger. "There," he said. "We're done."

Done? No. Despite the heartbreak and the anger and the distance, she could still see Ben getting out of the old station wagon, holding a puppy under his arm, smiling, wondering at her reaction, and she was on the front porch, shaking her head, wondering what he'd been thinking to come home with a puppy, and Jonathan, just five years old, was running across the lawn, laughing, and wondering if the puppy was theirs, and Ben, that night in bed with the puppy between them, finally quiet and asleep, saying, "How could I say, 'No?'"

Remember to Forget Me

Agnes screamed at him. She always screamed at him now, strident and jeering, like a blue jay warning him off. "Who are you? I know what you want! Don't touch me!" She clutched the yellow blanket to her breasts, then huddled against the flimsy headboard, the sheet tangled around her body, and her long, white hair flying past her shoulders. She spat at him again, as she often did, in emphasis. *Crazy old woman*, he thought, then, *beloved wife.*

He forgot before he remembered that she would always respond in this way.

He could remind Agnes, again, that they had been married for forty-six years, that they once had a daughter, Vivian, but no longer. That he was only adjusting the covers, being considerate, husbandly, keeping her well-being and safety in view.

"You see? Your feet? Your toes? They're freezing?" He can't help noticing the small, unintentional signs of neglect. Her toenails were long and curled over. *Hag's toes.* He wanted to be generous, let his glance glide away, but really, with the hair and the spit? Of course, in a world where his wife would sit still and allow the staff to clip the nails, where she wouldn't kick him as well, where bruises wouldn't bloom across his chest? But it was hard to be generous when she wouldn't even allow him to tug down the corner of her blanket.

Agnes glared at him and hugged her knees, like a recalcitrant child willful in her anger.

"It's me," he said, without expectation, but also without rancor. "Robert."

She shrugged and ran her hand through her hair. She had been adamant about keeping it long. The staff wanted to cut it short and Robert understood this. Thirty patients in the home, all needing showers and shaves and rudimentary grooming. Most were uncooperative. But this was a final realm over which she could exert control. He understood this, too.

Just last year, Agnes brushed and coiled her hair in a tight bun. At night, she sat on the edge of the bed, undressing, shirt first, then pants or skirt and hose, and then she turned her back to him; he ran his hands down her shoulders, across her warm skin, across the constellation of freckles and spots and the wrinkling after their decades together. Unhooked her bra. Unpinned her hair. He always wanted her. She sometimes wanted him, but just as often she pulled her nightgown over her head and pushed him away. Agnes.

She was in the home against his wishes by an intervention that was more of an ambush. He was out for his usual walk while Agnes napped and he locked her in the bedroom so she didn't light the apartment on fire or wander off into traffic. She'd already done both of those things, though only the kitchen curtains had gone up in flames and a stranger's car damaged while swerving to avoid her sudden appearance in the road. He returned from his walk to somebody from Social Services with a signed court order. They said they preferred to use reason over force. The document detailed his inability to take care of his wife. The document detailed the fact that his wife was now a danger to herself and others.

"Look, Robert," the caseworker said, pointing to the document's numbered sentences. He looked, squinting, but the letters collapsed on top of each other, refused to separate into the words that would separate him from his wife. How could he let them take Agnes from him? From their life together?

They had been sitting across from the neurologist on metal chairs with seats made of leather straps. For such a specialty, for such an unrelenting diagnosis, wouldn't more humane, forgiving seating be appropriate? A loveseat for proximity, for warmth, for a husband and wife, a mother and son, a father and daughter to cross hands, to allow their legs and shoulders to fall into each other, to support each other when the news broke them? All he could do, all Agnes could do, was grip the cold metal armrests.

The doctor spared little in the initial recitation of what would happen to her memory, to her brain, to her body, and he said it would happen quickly.

Agnes laughed. "Everyone relies on a GPS now. And there's Google which remembers everything." But she looked at her lap when she said this so Robert knew she understood.

They came home from the clinic with a binder of information and didn't speak for hours. Later, they held each other in bed like he and his brother did when their father thrashed around in the kitchen in his alcoholic rages, tossing chairs, breaking beer bottles, slapping their mother, threating to kill all of them; he and his brother knew they needed to hold each other and wait him out.

Finally, Agnes said, "So we heard the same thing. It will get bad. Unbearable. I know you love me. You know I love you. We must do the right thing for each other. I may not remember to save enough pills. You'll do this for me."

Robert thought about all he'd heard from the doctor. This was not a considered decision, but his wife would not get better. They would have to agree ahead of time when the when would be. If she couldn't, could he? How can love entertain this agreement?

He consented and then went to the bathroom, kneeled over the toilet, and got sick.

But like his father's drunkenness, he believed against reason, that this, too, might be a matter of waiting it out. The stubbornness of love. The flu, or some other passing virus. One morning or afternoon, his beautiful wife, yes, beautiful— more at seventy-five than twenty—the illness would pass in a fevered sweat and she would return. He still remembered the smooth arches of her feet, the swoop of copper hair swishing across her back like a paintbrush, how she looked at him when they made love, as if there was a tender, hilarious secret to the whole thing. The way she looked at him and recognized him, Robert, saw beyond the name, the flesh, the him that was hers. The way their daughter Vivian used to settle into her when she was a baby, caterwauling then soporific contentment.

The stubbornness of love. He let it go because it would have killed her. He would have killed his wife, which is what she had wanted. How could he feed her those pills when some days, some hours, some minutes she still looked at him with the recognition of love? Did it matter that she no longer knew his name? Did it matter that she no longer knew to find her way home to him? Did it matter that she pounded on the neighbor's door, hollering about an intruder in the house, and poor Mrs. LaSalle spent an hour beside Agnes on the couch explaining the intruder was no intruder but her husband, pointing to his photo, their photos together, and then at the very same sad man in the chair across the room?

One afternoon, sitting across the room from her, on one of those awful nursing home glider chairs, he wondered if maybe he shouldn't have just locked them both inside the apartment and turned on the gas. Agnes faced the window, relaxed, her chin resting on her knees, as if she was a girl contemplating summer camp, macramé bracelets, letters home to her parents still alive for fifty more years, wishing for a sister, a brother, a best friend, not a husband, not that, at least not before traveling the world and by world she imagined Brazil, Madagascar, China, Paris. And Robert had nothing to do with it yet, or at all, ever. From his coat pocket, his took out his sketch book and pencil, opened to a blank page, and tried to draw her

But too quickly she was standing and moving, pacing, and again, demanding, *Who are you? Who are you? Who are you?*

How to capture something in motion, alive, on the lifeless page? Maybe these were all amateur questions that could have been solved with some training, but he was an amateur after all. Granted, Agnes, would have said, an obsessed amateur. Sketchbooks always in his pockets, pages filled, and in the apartment, closets stacked with boxes of watercolors. As an inspector for the city, specializing in elevators and escalators, he was either smeared in grease or charcoal.

He painted landscapes, mostly, waveringly imprecise. But never just *land* or *scape*; never just the sandy beaches and ocean, never just the meadow looking over the lake, never just the yard deep with snow and a forgotten red tricycle poking out, but Agnes holding her straw hat to her head in the wind, knee-high in waves, and Agnes a distant whir in a bright orange cap, a buoy in the water, and Vivian stuffed into a green snowsuit, cramming snow into her mouth. He could never leave them out, depopulate the *land* for the sake of the *scape*.

But his paintings had no artistic value. Not for him. Agnes had kept them around. "Like photographs," she'd argued. "They capture us at a specific time."

"Watery blurs," he said.

She didn't care. The peachy splash in the murky water with the orange dot? "Unequivocally me." The green, wormy smudge in the pile of snow? "Indisputably Vivian. Ask anyone. Anyone, Robert. I don't know why you doubt yourself."

But he doubts himself. No one left, once he was gone, to say who was who and where was there. A guess, maybe, but filled with uncertainty. Amateur approximations. A wave, a tree, a hill, a sunrise, a sunset, a wife, a daughter. He would like to close shop. Condemn his old body with its rickety gears and slipshod fastenings, but he had promised to live alongside his wife. Parallel days, no longer shared. No, not parallel as nothing was shared between them anymore, and no one to pass it all down *to*—Vivian was thirty years dead. Still.

Still. That was the point. His daughter should be still in that grave but was always moving, always racing back and forth, mostly as a little girl.

"Daddy!" she shrieked, and came running towards him, abandoning her bicycle on the front lawn. One or two cold fingers poking through her woolen gloves which she pressed to his cheek as he pulled her to him.

"Did you keep people safe today?" she asked.

He gave her a kiss, as if sealing her safety. Then looked at his grease-blackened hands. Thirty-nine years on the job inspecting thousands of escalators and elevators which carried millions of people to the moon and back by now. And yet, there was no way to inspect Vivian's brain and the vessel that ballooned and burst while she was with her boyfriend in bed. "With"—the euphemism the college had used when they called. "Unclothed," they said, "when Vivian was found in Mr. Stephens's dormitory room." As Vivian's father, his first instinct was to blame the boyfriend, but Agnes in her grief held him back.

"They were making love, like we do. Nothing you could have done. All we can do is bear it."

Who does he share this frayed forbearance with now? Who else would ever know there was once a Vivian? Or an Agnes before this Agnes crouching at the head of the bed? Hopeless, fruitless, a cruel joke. And all the photographs he'd lined up on Agnes's bureau: their wedding photo taken on the steps of City Hall, Vivian's baby and high school graduation photos. Strangers, the whole lot of them. Agnes didn't even recognize herself. But then, he didn't recognize himself without her, without his wife to remember him and remind him who he had been, who he had wanted to be and all the small and large ways he had screwed up.

Even he can't remember without the benefit of their shared memory. Wasn't that the promise of the coming golden years, though he and Agnes were already beyond golf carts and glucosamine? If nothing else, their tandem wheelchairs should be pushed to a table by a window overlooking a swimming pool filled with the younger set playing geriatric water polo. Their lives might have been held between them like a deck of cards, playing as many games as possible—Go Fish, War, Crazy 8's. And then one random memory paired with the next, turns over the next, triggers the mind to go in search of the next: *Remember? What about that time? You really don't recall that? We were there, together. Can't you see it? What I would give to go back.*

After Agnes left the apartment, he sketched birds; it was impossible to see her inside that nursing home room. He tried looking at her, looking for her, but what materialized on the page through his pencil was blurry, smudged, as if he peered at her through leaded glass. Memory refusing to give way to reality.

At first, he traced over the birds in a worn copy of Audubon's *Birds of America*, getting a feel for their bodies, legs, feathers, beaks, and wings. A Trumpeter Swan paused, mid-paddle in quiet water, its long neck and beak swiveled towards a moth. Three Snow Buntings were no larger than sparrows, but on the page, in relief, were as great as the mountains behind them. The two on the ground waited for the one in flight to land and rest with them. Or maybe it was the reverse: maybe the one in flight called to the ones on the ground—*Follow me! Not safe! Don't rest yet!* Who could tell from a print almost two hundred years old, from birds stopped in flight?

Later, he went to the Natural History Museum and sat for hours in front of the displays, trying to capture the stuffed birds, birds that he would never see in his lifetime because he would never travel to China or the Amazon, birds no one would ever see again—the Ascension Night Heron, the Passenger Pigeon, the Mysterious Starling, the Great Auk.

Finally, he felt brave enough to try for the birds in the yard behind the apartment, in the parks around the city going about their bird business—the sparrows and blue jays, the robins and cardinals. It was a way to keep the hands nimble, to keep the eyes moving, searching, interested in the world of the still living. All those birds vanished in their migrations and returned, at least most of them, relying on the simple, mechanical wonder of winged flight. Like stripping down an escalator or elevator to see how it carried people up and down all day, year in and year out, to see all the nuts and bolts, all the cogs and wheels, what was necessary to grease and tighten.

He wondered what another artist, sketching the Passenger Pigeons, had thought when the birds failed to return that first year, and then the next, and then vanished. Like his daughter, disappearing from his sketchbooks and paintings. And now his wife.

The birds were pressing. More than a hobby. He was trying to understand something about flight. Not flight as in fleeing from, but flight as in movement through space. He was trying to sketch his birds in a way that revealed their *still moving*, not *still movement*, on the page. His sketchbook was filled with birds that looked like they dangled from bungee cords. Failure after failure. He had been a safety inspector, intent on careful, controlled, systematic movement. The mechanics of flight were easy. After all, there were manuals and diagrams. But what kept the bird in flight when it was tired, when it was far from land, far from shore? How did it remember to fly home to its nest? Was memory mechanical? Cogs and wheels, gears and grease? Merely for survival? To know home from exile, friends from strangers? And if so, to foster recognition and return, then why remember love and longing and loss? Why keep coming back to that again and again?

A nurse's aide entered with a towel and a plastic bin labeled "Agnes." He'd stocked the bin with Agnes's favorite shampoo, soap powder, and lotion, though from the grim look on the face of this aide, he doubted much time was ever given over to such niceties. He assumed it was enough of an epic feat just to give all the residents a basic wash down. Clinical necessity. Could Agnes remember Head and Shoulders Green Apple was her sensual necessity?

The shuffling of the deck. One summer Vivian took horseback riding lessons at a shoddy stable on the edge of the city. She was ten, maybe eleven, and a long brown braid hung to the middle of her back. Every Saturday morning, they drove out together, and she chattered on about the horses, about their different personalities, about their soft eyes and sweet nickers (never mind their rib cages showing through or the ziggurat manure piles in the stalls). She brought carrots and a giant bottle of lavender shampoo purchased with her allowance from the pharmacy (to wash off the horse at the end of the lesson). The stable was a mill, and every week she watched as the sweaty horse's belly was given a cursory spray with a hose before the next student climbed on.

One day, it was particularly humid and hot; the bees thumped around his legs as he stood with Vivian along the paddock fence watching the next group of girls at their lesson. He promised, as all fathers do, that one day he'd buy her a horse.

Vivian twirled a dandelion in her fingers. "That's okay. Mom already said she'd buy us a farm with as many horses as I can manage. I said four. One for each of us and whoever I marry." She flicked the mangled dandelion away. "You need to up the ante."

Her face was red and sweaty from the effort of the lesson, sunburned, too, and she held her velvet riding helmet under her arm in a way that suggested she could jump a steeplechase if she wanted. On her feet though, were black rubber rain boots. He and Agnes had argued with her for months. Leather riding boots were too expensive, especially for a first go around; she could make do for the summer. Oh, Vivian was angry, but more, (he understood in remembering this), was her embarrassment and shame, crossing her legs all the time, trying to hide those smelly rubber boots. If he could only remember Vivian leaning against that fence with her mussed up hair, her ruddy face, the beauty of that wilted dandelion flipping from one finger to the next, listening to her say, "Daddy," on repeat, "Daddy," if only he could remember this with Agnes who also knew Vivian best, remember her in gleaming, tall leather boots. Agony to go at this alone.

To look at Agnes and to know Agnes alone. To look in the mirror each morning as he shaved his face and remind himself that the face was his, Robert's, that it was a face in want of shaving, that Agnes would not recognize him with a beard, with grizzle, would only know him clean shaven because this was the face she had seen for their entire life together. Agony even if she cannot know him now? Even if she has fallen in love with another man?

Yes, goddammit, she had fallen in love with another man. There was still the remote chance, he had chosen to cling to this, that somewhere in the plaques and tangles of her nerves and cells, there were, if not the photographs, then the negatives of their life together—there were, if not the feelings of love spoken and felt year after year, then the echoes reverberating on the tongue and fingers.

The news came without warning. But then, all news does.

"You are not him," Agnes had said one morning. She was on the edge of the bed, one leg wrapped around the other, one foot on the ground tap-tap-tapping. The word that came to mind was *coiled*. "No," she said, and shook her head again, "you are not him."

José pushed past him, bearing a bouquet of tissue paper flowers taped to painted Popsicle sticks. "My lovely," he said to his wife, "these are for you." And this man, this José, reached down and kissed his wife on the cheek.

His wife, his Agnes sprang up and wrapped her thin arms around this small man and she whispered something to José that was meant to be only for this man but because Robert was standing near the bed, and because his wife no longer remembered he was her husband and that she loved him and that he mattered and likely that he was even in the room, Robert heard Agnes say, "You are here, finally. All this time I've been waiting for you."

He should have left the room then. When Agnes was at home, he kept wondering, bad enough? Should he wait, keep watch, get through it together for one more month, week, day, night, hour, minute, meal? Like that, he was caught, watching Agnes and this trespasser, waiting for the moment when it would all go wrong, when her fog would lift. Should he call out for the staff?

"Help! Help me! Help her!"

What sort of redress did he want? His wife and this José, what were they doing? Sitting on the edge of the bed in their flimsy bathrobes, holding hands, admiring paper flowers Vivian might have once made for them in kindergarten?

He overstayed his unwelcome because at that moment Agnes, likely drawing on the now unconscious echoes of their long-standing love to foster this connection between her now unknown self and this unknown (though for-the-record-named-José) suitor, turned to her husband, and said, "Whoever you are, leave or I'll call the police! Or my husband will." She nudged José, who nodded, and she added, "He means business."

Who could take José seriously with his orange juice stained bathrobe, a tooth brush poking out of the breast pocket, and a big toe poking through his slipper? He decided to wait him out.

It was strange to watch his wife in love with another man, to see joy suffuse her face when this José entered the room with his gifts of origami swans and toilet paper roll telescopes which they used to look at the sunsets.

"Don't worry," the Director said, "this happens all the time. The residents are together twenty-four hours a day, so it is often inevitable. And if we can be generous," the Director waited for him to agree with this obligation before continuing, "then we must allow that it helps to mitigate your wife's loneliness and isolation."

The social worker assured him that it was nothing more than a schoolyard crush, just hand-holding and the odd chaste kiss. "We monitor everything. Besides," she laughed, "I doubt most of them would remember how to get it done. The men are on so many meds, they would have difficulty."

As if this tactless mocking of the varieties of loss was supposed to assure him. "My wife loves another man," he wanted to remind her, "as in Waits on the Edge of Her Bed for Him but Not for Me. As in, Spits at Me, Doesn't Recognize Me from Adam, but José Over There is Her Mario Lanza."

In the art museum, he walked around a vase for a long time not because he was particularly interested in ceramics, but for the swallows. The vase was at least three feet tall, mostly a creamy yellow; the limbs of a tree grew around the curve with its wide, green leaves, and three swallows in flight. If he stood in place, looking at the vase head on, he could only see one bird, and the wings of the other two, so flight halted. But if he walked around it, the swallows kept appearing and disappearing, as if in flight.

Maybe his understanding was obvious, limited by his sketchbook and abilities. Doubtful he'd throw any pots unless he went to one of those paint-your-own-clay-unicorn places for kids. But these swallows flying around the curves showed him that there was no end to their flight. Despite the closed form—a vase not the sky—it was boundless movement. The swallows would circle around, again and again, but only if he walked with them and continued to track their migration. His was an inadequate, clumsy human flight, but necessary to track the birds who disappeared and the birds who flew on, their feathers always out of reach along the curve.

He bought scrubs from a uniform supply store. So many possible prints—balloons, circus animals, smiley faces, even birds. When he told the nursing staff his plan, they were happy to make him a name tag which he affixed to his top.

Now, he comes in each day, wearing his bird print scrubs and name tag, and walks into his wife's room and waits. He walks around the room, sometimes raising the shade, straightening the chair, feeling her watch him, but stays silent.

"Who are you?" Agnes finally says with suspicion.

"I'm Robert," he says, "here to help you with whatever you need."

She nods, though mostly spits at him. Sometimes she lets him help with her shower. He is anonymous now, no longer a threat, no longer insisting on claiming her as his. He runs his fingers through the long tangle of her white hair, working at the knots, feeling the ridges of her skull, where beneath, are those memories locked away—a life of Robert and Agnes and Vivian and before Robert and Agnes and Vivian. Or maybe just gone now, just the emptiness. A new love in its place? Then she pulls away. But it is something. More than what he'd had.

After? He often thinks of Vivian in her last lovely moments. Of course, he can't know with any certainty if those moments were lovely but that is what he tells himself. Vivian happy, maybe ecstatically so, before her awful end. And Agnes? This, too, is an awful end, and it will get even worse. But why not fly alongside and ease her suffering and despair? Besides, there is no one left to remember the love that came before except for him.

No, *she* is not in despair. Once she crossed over from remembering into forgetting for good, *she* has been able to love again. *He* has been the one in despair. Page through the sketchbooks from the year. As if he had been drawing with the nub of a pencil and reduced to outlining signs of a coming extinction. He could not draw Agnes at all. Only feathers and bones and scattered egg shells. Nothing left and nothing coming back. But it has come back, hasn't it, in paper flowers and toilet paper tubes?

Now, he draws Agnes and José seated on the bench in the garden, their bodies pressed against each other, shoulders to shoulder, his hand on her thigh, her face tilted toward the sky. On her lap, another bouquet of paper flowers, orange and purple carnations. Their slippers are kicked off under the bench and they alternate between scuffing their feet in the grass and then entwining them around each other.

In another life, a version he can hardly remember he wanted, he would sit beside his wife on a bench like this in a park, their daughter across from them, perhaps with a family of her own—didn't she want a husband?—so a husband, and a son and a daughter, and four horses grazing in the grass. He is going to ask for it all. Because here he is, wearing scrubs and a nametag, chaperoning his wife and her new temporary husband. There is a birdbath beside the bench. *Ssshhh*, he says, and everybody goes quiet and looks to where he points. A pair of passenger pigeons drinks from the water; their gray feathers and rosy breasts shimmer in the sun. They are tired and thirsty and though lost for many years, they did not forget their way back to the home they loved for so long.

Humiliation, In Parts

Nigel's leaving was unimaginative and cruel. "Fortunately," he said, "I don't love you anymore. You must know that, Melina." Did he really sigh in exasperation, as if long-beleaguered by my now official marginal presence in his life?

I was bent over, balanced on my hands and feet, butt raised in the air, in Downward Dog.

Sunday morning. The day after his brother's marriage to Caroline, the newest, thinnest, youngest wife yet. But for Nigel's brother Paul, a securities analyst, it was not difficult to hedge bets on yet one more permutation of the future: Ashley, the pedigreed Contemporary Art appraiser traded for Monika, the German Model/Barista/Reflexologist traded for Caroline, a VP in Mergers and Acquisitions schooled in the art of making and taking money.

But Nigel? A number-crunching actuary? Three hours of sleep and ten glasses of champagne. Surely, he was still drunk. But that sigh, without pity, was a warning: *don't beg, don't snivel, no scene though that is what you will make anyway.* After all, as an actuary, he was distanced from the emotional appeal, an adroit manager of catastrophe. Isn't risk always a matter of perspective? What is harmful to one party is good for another and vice versa. I would be hurt so he could be happy.

I noticed, now that I was no longer upside-down, now that my head was out of my ass, that he still wore the remnants of his tuxedo, the anonymous, impersonal uniform. Any husband leaving any wife.

"You can't leave. Not now," I said stupidly. "Italy is next week." As if the mere reminder would summon up a future so powerful (simultaneous coin toss into the Trevi Fountain? Chianti by sunset beneath an olive tree? Intermezzi intercourse al fresco?), he'd reconsider: *I meant to say, I don't love your smeared lipstick on the water glasses or that flannel granny nightgown.*

"That's why I can't go through with it." He stood in front of the window, fiddling with the hotel blinds. Open. Shut. Open. Shut. Open.

"*It* meaning me. You can't go to Italy with me."

He nodded in brutal confirmation. Against the benevolent light of morning, his round face was suddenly angular—nose, chin, and brows in sharp relief, all soft sentiment stripped away like an impersonal Cubist statue with hard geometry replacing compassion.

And then I knew. "But with someone else?"

Which was how I found out about Lydia, the woman he now loved. He didn't seek her out, he explained, he didn't seek anyone out. She just happened.

Oh, pardon me, Nigel, while I pull the knife from your heart. It just happened to stab you. "No passive voice allowed in love or leaving," I said.

"But Melina," he said, "don't you agree that our life together is a series of diminishing returns? Do you want to become people with nothing to talk about besides diapers, dog farts, and septic systems?"

"All hypotheticals," I pointed out. "No kid, no dog, no house. Just us and our apartment. And why we decided on Italy. You said we were reinvesting in our marriage." I sobbed, called him names—*Motherfuckersonofabitch*—begging him not to do this though he already had. But I also hovered on the outside of it all, clinical and detached from my own sad-sack-hysterical-self, assessing how far I would go to keep a man who no longer wanted to keep me. Did I throw my coffee cup at him? Did it hit him on the shoulder? Did I slap him?

Nigel blotted at the dark stain on his shirt with a towel. "As for Italy," he said, all composure, because of course, he'd been rehearsing the conversation for months already, "you go. It's bought and paid for."

Briefly, I considered hurling myself from the window. Ten floors down, a mashed head and broken heart. My disembodied, disemboweled spirit would flit around his prostrate, weeping form, jabbing him in the side, flicking the backs of his ears. Now clean up your mess, I'd whisper. But then the other image intervened: he might weep for a bit, but he wouldn't be disconsolate; rather, Lydia would buoy him up with her strong shoulder and warm embrace.

He slipped on his tuxedo jacket, picked up a fat, pre-packed duffel bag, and left. Lydia had already booked him an earlier flight back to Chicago. I wasn't so stupid to believe that the mere fact we were still having sex was any proof of love or genuine longing, especially since it often seemed perfunctory: in bed, under the sheet, switching who's-on-top-performative places, waiting each other out as we stared mutely at *The Late Show* and its stupid pet tricks: a monkey riding on the back of a dog; a goat dancing the merengue; a parrot pecking seed from its owner's tongue. All more interesting than sex, or at least, sex with me.

But there had been no real abatement, no change in his end satisfaction or mine, in our mutual, official satisfaction. We were, I assumed, temporarily lost in the era of the quickie, the swath of time occupying the center of long-standing marriages, as many of my friends concurred. More imaginative, prop-reliant, acrobatic sex? When you're thirty-eight and otherwise distracted with breast-feeding or toilet training, in vitro fertilization or pre-adoption trips to China and Ethiopia? With apartment expansions and renovations or relocations to pearly-gated suburbs with their zoning laws, paint scheme regulations, and official lawn heights? Just eight months earlier wasn't I doubled-over and bleeding out, for the second time in two years, our hoped-for baby? Didn't Nigel kneel beside me, and whisper it would all be okay, we would get through it together, we'd try again and again and again, however long to make our two, three?

Now we were three.

What I had imagined back at home, before Nigel left, when we still innocently grazed our way through scrambled eggs, wheat toast, strawberry jam, and coffee was a small wooden table under an olive tree, cappuccino topped with a swirl of steamed milk, and biscotti. Dark saucer-sized sunglasses, hair swept into a neat chignon, a blue flowered skirt made of lawn cotton, the scalloped hem skimming my calves, cinched tight at my waist. And Nigel in a slim seersucker blazer and stark white shirt, one hand holding a tiny cup of espresso, the other balanced on the back of my neck. And there, right beneath the tree, I would feed him fat, dark grapes and he would lick my thighs, and we would be the best of lovers again.

I thought I knew Nigel: same job, same haircut, same turkey on wheat, every day, for fifteen years. His routine was a soothing pseudo-assurance and its steady rhythm felt like a life. When did he deviate? I searched for evidence. Illicit letters under the mattress? Red thongs in a coat pocket? A hotel receipt in the nightstand? Only pennies and nickels, nail clippers, wadded up tissues, cards from me to him—*Happy Valentine's Day! Happy Birthday! Happy Anniversary! Twelve Years of Happiness!* Bland professions of mediocre affection. I should have done better. After all, I'd once written an article for *Cosmopolitan* on The World's! Greatest! Love Notes! Beethoven: "I can only live, either altogether with you or not at all." Johnny Cash: "The fire may be gone now... but the ring of fire still burns around you." Even Sid Vicious wrote Nancy a list of her attributes more specific than I could write for Nigel: "Witty. Fab taste in clothes. Sexy feet. The most beautiful wet pussy in the world."

I sat with my black carry-on in the terminal, watching other travelers, pairs, gather for my flight. Despite the humiliation, I still longed for Nigel. He could even have the window seat, just so we could step off the plane together into Italy and say: *Molto bene madre puttanesca amore Inglese ciao!* And maybe, when we made love, it would be slower and more profound because we'd just seen David and wandered the Piazza Navona and the taste of salty prosciutto was on our lips. I texted—"Come with me. Let's try."—and waited for the buzz back, though immediately regretting my impulsive prostration. But still: unguarded hope. Maybe he'd appear on the tarmac, waving down the plane, beseeching me for forgiveness.

· · ·

Forgiveness. That was what my Buddhist-lite therapist said I should begin to work on when I SOS-called her after Nigel left. That and Gratitude.

"It's only been three days," I said.

"I want you to thank him," she said, her voice even and placid. I imagined Debra in her reproduction Eames chair, blue silk blouse tucked snugly under the waistband of a black skirt, one leg crossed over the other, black patent stiletto dangling off the toe of her suspended foot.

"Thank him for fucking another woman? For lying?" I was standing at the window in the apartment, forehead pressed against the glass. The light had changed. Afternoon. Hours immobile in bed. I watched the people below scuttling down the street. How many were liars and cheats?

Debra breathed in and out, in and out. Was I meant to breathe too? "The practice of gratitude is challenging," she finally said. "Begin now."

Another pause. Then what sounded like tapping on a keyboard? Was she typing notes from her previous session? The typing paused.

"Where are you going, Melina? And how will you get there?" She hung up on the cryptic platitude.

Forgive Nigel already? Release my anger—breathe in, breath out—just like blowing frothy white seeds from a dandelion's head? Nigel wasn't coming back and I wasn't going to Italy to discover my gratitude in pasta, parmesan, and prayer.

At Hotel Galileo, the concierge leered as he took my passport and then handed me the bulky room key. No easy swipe card, and judging by the crush at the elevator, only one couple with luggage per ascent. Easier to haul mine up the three flights.

"Kiril," the concierge said, "I make your stay nice." Eastern European accent, hair shorn, broad nose as if repeatedly broken, slathered in astringent cologne.

"Thank you," I said.

"Mr. Philips must give passport." His eyes slid from me, scanning the crowded lobby.

"Just me," I said and held steady.

While he studied my passport, writing down my information, I looked at the map open on the desk.

"I can show you the most best places," Kiril said. "Maybe you like to dance and drink whiskey?"

"I have the tour," I said.

He shrugged. "You sign, please. And no illegal guests." He leaned into me. "But I not tell anyone if you do."

Room 306. Two single beds pushed together. And in their middle, as if to bridge the gap, two white towel swans surrounded by paper rose petals. I shoved the swans to the floor, where they unfurled, neck over body, stretched out on one of the beds, and stared at the water-stained ceiling tiles.

I slept straight through to morning. No small disappointment when I saw Hotel Galileo's breakfast: urn of tepid coffee, platter of cold, slick ham and bland, white cheese, basket of stale rolls, artificial juice in an automatic dispenser, and bruised apples, and reflected over and over in wall-to-wall, faux gilded mirrors. Most of the touring couples were chatty and intimate already, trading the duplicative facts of their lives: home— Cleveland, Milwaukee, Fort Wayne; grandchildren—Ohio State, UW, Indiana State; pounds lost in advance of pounds gained slurping fettuccini alfredo and chocolate gelato—none, but they tried in Zumba. Groups of four at tables for four. One empty table in the corner, and though I had no food, I sat down with the awful coffee. The tour would move from Rome to Tuscany, from Hotel Galileo to Villa Macelli's promise of fresh squeezed juice, rustic bread, apricot marmalade, marscapone, and warm, hard boiled eggs.

I gulped at my coffee and took in the room. The Good Ship Lollipop. Husbands and wives coordinated: men in polos, khakis, and sneakers; women in sleeveless polos, scarves, capris, and sneakers. More après golf then avant Rome.

"Let's just go on a trip where we don't have to think about anything," Nigel had said. We were jogging in the park, though Nigel's jog was more sprint, and I was always trying to catch up. In retrospect, he'd been leaving me in many little ways, but at the time, I believed that if I could keep pace, we would be fine: huff and puff, shower, make love. When I fell behind? He'd disappear down the path while I caught my breath and by the time I got home, he was sprawled on the couch watching football. He'd say, "Fall in the lake again?" No emergency, no worry, just the flat acknowledgment that I had fallen behind and he wasn't waiting for me to catch up. Where was the solicitude? His fingers on my arm drawing a figure eight, and after the last miscarriage, washing the blood from my thighs, and the murmurs of loving reassurance as we drifted off to sleep? No exact date pinpointing their end; just a gradual petering out of relational gestures.

Nigel wanted the tour company. "I don't have time to plan. And what do we know about Italy? This way we'll see everything without the hassle."

We'd used a travel agent for Paris and every other vacation was to a guarded, mega-compound resort in the Caribbean. Surely, we weren't imbeciles?

Nigel kept the jog to a jog.

"I've looked at the itinerary," he said, and even rested his hand on my shoulder for a half a stride. "Wandering around Rome. Then a Tuscan Villa. Can't you see it?"

I didn't see anything at all. Nigel failed to mention that Lydia booked the tours on commission.

"Are these seats taken?"

A woman: pink polo shirt and white capris, an enormous triple-looped rope of plastic pearls around her neck and a plate of food in her hands. Short hair, Midwestern efficient, dyed a shocking red. Her husband: blue polo and brown pants, balding and overweight, a plate balanced on his palm.

"Yours," I said, without enthusiasm.

"Nan," she said.

"Bob," he said.

"Melina."

Bob ate his meat and cheese sandwich in two bites. Nan spread butter and marmalade across the stale roll, then pulled out four packets of Sweet 'n Low from her purse.

"Never go anywhere without them," she said. "Yesterday, breakfast in Cleveland and today Rome. Where did you have your last coffee?"

"Instant Nescafé isn't coffee, and certainly not the cappuccino in the brochure," I said.

Nan shrugged. "All I need is a kickstart. Where are you from?"

"Chicago," I said. Already I was tired of talking.

Bob looked up from the map he'd unfolded across his plate. "On the move today. The Forum, Colosseum, Pantheon, Spanish Steps, Piazza Navona, and Trevi Fountain. There'd better be pizza and pasta. I'm here to eat."

"Does yours give you trouble?" Nan said.

I shook my head.

"Late sleeper? Jet lag is awful," Nan said.

"He's not here. Not here at all."

"He's all right?" Nan was nodding but I wasn't nodding back.

Where would Nigel be if he was here? Not sleeping in, not jetlagged. One look at the dining room and he'd head for a café with a counter and espresso and Italians. He wouldn't have settled for a Lunchables breakfast.

But Nigel wasn't whispering to me in the café across from Hotel Galileo, was he? *Per sempre, per sempre.* I was alone, and Nigel back home, whispering to Lydia, *Ti amo, ti amo, ti amo,* to Lydia.

"He's fine," I said, "if fine means screwing another woman in Chicago."

Nan looked pained. At the terrible coffee? At my too-soon confidence? But then she said, matter-of-factly, "The thing to do is to show him that you are just fine without him and you can always sit with us."

Day Two: The Vatican. While imagining Nigel in hell was appealing, another day crammed in the tour bus, herded two by two by two in a line was not. I went off-tour to the Galleria Borghese hoping for the blessed silence of Bernini, Raphael, Caravaggio as opposed to the prattle of my tour mates oohing and aahing over the Vatican's bedazzled glitz and a self-serve steam table at Pasta Dante, wine not included.

But just as many besotted tourists jostling me in the hallways and rooms of the museum, though I was equally besotted. Canova's "Pauline Bonaparte"—Pauline lying on her bed of marble, her naked body draped in cloth, one arm propped casually behind her head, the other lying across her hip holding an apple. Bernini's "Apollo and Daphne"—Daphne becoming a laurel tree; Apollo's hand on her body, feeling the cool marble of her still beating heart. Caravaggio's "David With the Head of Goliath"—David matter-of-factly wiping the bloodied blade across his tunic, and holding Goliath's head like a lantern.

But it was Cranach's, "Venus and Cupid with a Honeycomb," on loan from somewhere else, that held me still. The beautiful, naked Venus was under a transparent veil while baby Cupid sucked on a stolen honeycomb, realizing, too late, that it was full of bees. At the top of the canvas, a Latin inscription translated in the painting's notes: "*Voluptas*, pleasure, is always transitory and mixed with pain." Perhaps Lydia's allure was her novelty: her expressions and reactions still charmingly unpredictable, and her blow jobs willing and spontaneous. But no doubt about it. One day, the bees would sting Nigel.

"You like this painting?"

A line—it had to be one—from the mouth of a youngish Italian man. Did I care? He was looking at me rather than the painting.

I shrugged. "The beginning and end of desire. What's to like?"

He smiled and waved his hand. "The beginning is best. The end is pain. I would not wish for you pain."

"Always when there's an end. See? Bees hiding in the honeycomb." I was pointing at Cupid but staring at his smile. Ridiculous, a cliché because I knew what was next. This was the antidote to Nigel and his tour operator, to their fucking in her bed, to his mouth on hers, to him choosing her over me. I would get Luigi or Giovanni or Guiseppe and too much red wine on the Spanish Steps and fantastico sex. Who cared if this was the Italiano modus operandi with American women? I could pretend that I was his one and only for the night, like I pretended with Nigel for years that what we had was love instead of chips and beer at the 24-Hour convenience store.

Only that's not how it went down with Marco, if that was his name. We wandered around the museum flirting and I feigned hard to get since the chase is the seduction. Instead of the Spanish Steps, he took me to a dingy narrow bar down a dubious side street. No tables, just men drinking murky beer and smoking one cigarette after another. The bartender slid a carafe of red wine in front of us along with two spotty glasses. We drank three carafes. Marco whispered, "Sei bellissima, sei bellissima. Voglio scopare," and ran his hand down my back and over my ass, pulling me to him. What could I do? I wanted to be wanted.

His apartment was a dump. Even drunk, I could see that. Dirty dishes piled in the kitchen. Dead plants along the windowsill. Ratty futon that he pulled out into a bed. No turning back though because I was going to show Nigel, even though he wouldn't see it, that I was onto something greater, something *molto romantico.*

Marco kicked off his clothes. I folded mine in a neat pile.

No sheet on the futon. I avoided looking at the stains.

Marco said, "You need to be in, how you say, doggie?"

There it was—for the sake of getting one over on Nigel, I let myself have it. While Marco, or whatever his name was, grunted behind me, I stared at the saffron wall imagining the tour group couples cozied up in the hotel's hard, narrow beds, two-by-two, tired after a long day at the Vatican, contemplating heaven and hell, angels and devils, martyrs and sinners, soul and eternity, God and Man, and at Pasta Dante, too much lasagna and not enough wine. Some even making love, sweet, rousing, mundane but not empty love, not after all that'd seen that day, and none being fucked by a gigolo shouting Italian expletives.

I rolled away from Marco.

He puckered his eyebrows, wounded.

"The end is pain," I said. "Remember?"

Villa Macelli was picturesque. The sunburned stucco was crumbling though maybe that was deliberate, part of the roughed-up, old-world charm. The stone fountain was filled with stagnant water and in the middle, a naked statue, a woman, with one hand draped over her head and the other supporting her breasts which were meant to spurt water. A rusty old Fiat, missing its wheels, was parked under the shade of a cypress tree.

The bus blared its horn and the driver announced over the microphone, as if we didn't already know, "Arrivato!"

Nan stood up, stretched, checked that both white hoops were still in her ears, and said, "We're going to have to make the best of it."

"As long as there's wine," I said, enough to blot out Nigel and Lydia and whatever I imagined they did in bed, enough to blot out Marco riding me roughshod and me letting him and that wall in front of me, and enough to blot out feeling like I'd been thrown out and used up and I'd been the one to let it happen. Buckets of wine might keep things at a steady hum, my feet in the olive groves, hands in the grape vines, face tipped to the sunshine. I could talk to Nan and Bob about bowling, casseroles, lawn mowing, and whether marriage gets better when you weather the storms and how do you do that and is it even worth hoping for it again?

Nan kissed Bob's bald head. "C'mon," she said. "It'll be fine."

"A shithole," he said. "A scam. Like a rundown B & B off I-80."

"Then we might as well have shithole wine," Nan said. "They make their own and we don't have to worry about drunk driving."

Bob ambled down the bus after her, a hand on her back. A point of connection. That's all I was after—sustained mutual regard and tenderness. In the courtyard, a few hardscrabble chickens pecked in the dust. In the distance, a tractor idled. On the edge of the fountain, a tray stacked with yellow blossoms.

I walked over and picked one up and sniffed. Nothing. Just vegetable matter.

"You don't smell it, you stuff it and eat it," a voice said. New York accent.

I turned.

A wiry woman with cropped, dark hair in dusty jeans, a washed-out tee-shirt, and Birkenstocks held a bowl of cherry tomatoes. "Zucchini flower. It's dinner. Try this." She gave me a tomato.

Warm. Sweet. Candy. But the cook was American? What happened to Nonna with the rolling pin and gnocchi and breasts that fed a nation? We were getting an ex-pat who learned Chicken Parm at the Culinary Institute?

"Not what you expected, right?" she said. "Not like those mealy ones you get in the States. You don't need to do anything to these except eat them." She nodded at her own pronouncement and then gave me a handful. "Eat and you'll feel better about everything. Even the pool which is slimed up with algae. I'm Glenda," she said.

"Melina," I said.

"Follow me," she said.

We walked into the kitchen.

"You had a rough one. Rome is brutal." She poured something clear into a glass and handed it to me.

I drank it down and coughed.

"Grappa," she said. "Homemade. That should help you forget last night. One more should erase it." She tipped the bottle over the glass.

"I thought you were supposed to be in a housedress and slippers."

She laughed. "I was at The Olive Garden in Orlando making Chicken Toscana two hundred times a day. My girl-friend broke up with me so why not learn to cook for real? I've been here ever since. Why are you here with the Midwest Express?"

"My husband wanted easy. As in, the travel agent, so I got the tour. A little weird—a lot weird—could I have another glass?—being on the couples tour as a single, but I met a guy in Rome."

"Awful?"

I sighed. "I'm mostly intact. But look at this food."

Glenda nodded. "Liver pâté crostini, stuffed zucchini blossoms, fennel and pecorino salad, lemon risotto with peas, lambchops, and gelato. Better than the endless soup and salad bar."

Even though we were only staying two nights before moving on to Florence, the room in its shabby, singular charm demanded that I unpack: the eight-foot armoire with the veneer peeling from its doors like an onion skin; the mirrored vanity with so many cracks it was as if it was made for a carnival funhouse; a badly chipped fresco of a beatific Christ on the cross, who looked, despite his profusely bleeding wounds, quite at peace with the indignities suffered upon him. But no table, no luggage stand. Was I supposed to leave my enormous suitcase, meant to hold clothes for two, on the floor? I unpacked.

I no longer had any utilitarian pajamas. An idiotic blurb of wisdom I'd read in some magazine regarding resuscitating failing marriages: no sweatpants or tee-shirts to bed, only sexy, fetching lingerie. To prevent backsliding, I pitched all my schlumpy bedwear in favor of hopeful chemises, babydolls, and teddies, but I might as well have been wearing a coffee-stained flannel onesie for all Nigel noticed. He had accounts to manage, emails to answer, and Lydia to text.

Only my sweet nothing to bring along: pink, silk chemise edged in Chantilly lace. On a Sophia Loren impulse, I took off my skirt, shirt, and bra and slipped it on over my head. No full-length mirror in the room. Not that I needed to see myself: not fat or thin, beautiful or ugly, wit or bore, stalker or church mouse. But it felt different wearing it here than in Hotel Galileo where it had felt like I was waiting up for the Nigerian busboy. Here, Jesus looked down upon me with a knowing smile—all would be well.

I laid back on the bed and ran my hand down the silk, over my body, between my legs, lingering there.

The door suddenly opened. A short, fat woman with a cleaning trolley and her mouth open and her hands raised in protest. "Mi scusi, mi scusi!" she said, and backed out, closing the door.

I rolled towards the wall. What I wanted—who I wanted—or the only person I could imagine wanting—was Nigel. Enough muscle memory left to summon up what we had been like earlier on, and what that was? Good enough, happy enough, loving enough. So that right now, that earlier Nigel would have—might have—pulled me to him and said not to worry about the housekeeper or Marco (would I see them back in America?)—these are not catastrophes—keep it in perspective—will you care in one year? in five? in ten? I wanted that Nigel back, the Nigel of our probable future, who, on the day he asked me to marry him, had said he had calculated the likelihood of our future happiness and it was a zero-risk investment.

In the middle of the courtyard, another non-operational fountain slick with green mold: an enormous stone lion at inexplicable rest; paws crossed, tail wrapped around its body, mouth opened without cause. No prey in its open jaw which was lit by a flickering candle. Spindly topiaries were festooned with twinkly lights. Once again, tables for four. At the back table, near the kitchen, the bus driver and tour director sat with a carafe of red wine, smoking and shaking their heads at one another. Not there. I thought about retreating to my room but Nan waved me over.

I tried to smile.

"You missed the wine tasting in the cellar," she said, pouring me a glass from the carafe.

"I made sure to get my money's worth from that wine waiter. He kept trying to pour these Mickey Mouse glasses," Bob said.

I closed my eyes and took a sip, letting the wine fill my mouth.

"I kept telling you, that's what a tasting is. A taste. A little bit of everything. Not a lot of a lot. And you're supposed to spit out what you drink. Right, Melina? You've got the big city know-how."

I took another sip, a big one, in answer.

"Then how the hell are you supposed to get drunk?" Bob said.

Nan swatted him. He winked at her.

I poured myself another glass. "How long have you been married?"

"Eighteen years," Nan said.

"Sometimes it feels like fifty," Bob said. "Sometimes a day."

The waiter brought the first course: liver pâté crostini. Still warm, creamy, peppery, a little metallic. Washed down with a glass of wine. I poured another.

"It gets better," Bob said.

"What does?" I asked.

"You're all jittery and wary and not yourself and wondering when it all stops being like this. I had it, too, when my first wife left me." He took a bite of the crostini and wiped his mouth with the back of his hand. "But you'll be okay. You do stupid things, but then you find your way again. Right, Nan? Stupid shit."

The next course arrived: zucchini blossoms stuffed with ricotta and mint.

Nan said, "He almost married somebody else."

"She was from Russia and she was going to pay me but I had to agree to no sex." Bob looked at his plate. "What is this thing? A jalapeño popper? I mean, how could I agree to that?

Being married but not married? And so desperate I had to pay somebody to marry me? No deal. And it got better after that and it will get better for you."

I finished my glass and poured another. "I wish I could pay somebody to make it better."

"Oh honey," Nan said, "just go to the nail salon and get someone to rub your hands and feet for an hour."

The waiter refilled the carafe.

Nan was asleep in her clothes from the night before in my bed on top of the covers. I was under the covers, naked, head pounding, mouth parched.

I sat up. My dress and underpants were folded on the floor. I nudged Nan.

"Oh," she said quickly, without any bleary effort, "I've been waiting. How are you feeling?" She sat at the end of the bed.

I shrugged. "Terrible. I remember salad but it ends there. That can't be good."

"Ignorance can be bliss."

"I take it I didn't hide out in my room."

Nan shook her head. "It was dramatic. Right around the risotto you started shouting you wanted to shove the wine bottles up the behinds of your husband and his mistress. You painted a realistic picture. Then you said your husband was missing out on what you had to offer and that a certain Roman appreciated your finer points." Nan looked up at Jesus. "Isn't he unnerving?"

"Only when I'm getting dressed, so I turn my back on him. But if you believe in the whole business, he's seen it all, right?" Nan didn't laugh.

Instead she said, "I'm sorry, Melina, you went Lady Godiva. Bob and I tried to stop you but you went Bruce Lee, too."

I stared at Jesus who stared back.

"You stood on the chair and took off your dress and panties and kept shouting and then you grabbed your knife and ran off into the olive grove. We ran after you, but everyone was drunk, and to be honest, you're probably twenty years younger than everyone. The chef caught up with you and convinced you to come back to the room. I stayed to make sure you were safe."

"How could I? That's not me," I said, my face turning red and hot with shame.

"Wine helps. A lot of wine. And a cheating husband," Nan said. "But the way back is not through wrack and ruin."

I'd taken flight with my smashed heart because I was sure our friends knew about the affair before me, knew that I'd been played the fool, still believing my marriage could be salvaged. I was stupid and didn't know it but they did. Nigel certainly did. Faux-marriage: we'd sat on our imitation mid-century modern couch (invented color: *putty*, though more cement but who pays two grand for mortar?), watching reality shows about naked people voluntarily starving on remote islands, while he'd been thinking "Fess up tonight?" Or while holding his dick for a pee, (just hours earlier in Lydia's hands), thinking, "Now?" Or in the run-up to Italy, while listening to my chatter about tiramisu, did he imagine running away with Lydia to a Saskatchewan love igloo?

Had we ever made a life together? We'd been married, stayed married when so many friends had divorced. We were reasonably man and wife: I swept up my stray hairs from the bathroom floor, he wiped down the sink after shaving, and we assiduously deposited money into our retirement accounts for a house on St. John's instead of a condo on the Panhandle.

What I'd needed on this trip were strangers who knew nothing about me, about Nigel, about any of it, but now everyone knew that I was someone who had been left and was no longer loved.

A knock at the door.

Glenda held a tray: orange juice, bread, cheese, jam, a glass with flowers. "I didn't think you'd be ready for your fans."

"I'm sorry. I don't get drunk, not like that."

"I've been there," Glenda said. "I used to drive past my ex's house and watch her and her new girlfriend through the window all happy on the couch. She caught me and called the cops. On me, the person she used to love. I had to get away." Glenda handed over the tray. "We do crazy things when we get hurt. Sometimes we do them to ourselves."

I stood at the edge of the foundering pool. Walls slick in green slime, and on the bottom, an enormous blue and green mosaic star missing most of its blue and yellow tiles. I imagined swimming back and forth through the water, looking down at that ruined universe. Nigel was an incompetent actuary. Zero risk? He'd bankrupted both investors. But when irritation and anger superseded accommodation and forgiveness? We shouldn't have waited each other out, but told each other when love ended. Wasn't it more humiliating waiting alone in bed, again, past midnight, the other half of the bed undisturbed since Nigel was out with "clients"? Wasn't that more humiliating than standing naked at the pool's edge, hung over, but swimming through the water and the muck for that star?

The Lionman

In the evening, Dreamland hummed under one million incandescent bulbs strung across its streets like tethered stars. Tens of thousands arrived by steamship from terminals in Manhattan and Harlem, jammed the promenades and exhibition halls, and jostled each other to see the corralled Wild Men of Borneo chanting their strange, guttural songs. Or Zip the What-Is-It Pinhead plucking haplessly at his banjo and hopping from foot to foot. Or the Lilliputia dwarves in their scale model town of fifteenth-century Nuremburg with its own parliament, fire engines responding hourly to false alarms, and a Chinese laundryman washing, ironing, and folding small clothes into fastidious, warm stacks. Two-hour lines for the Airships, the Ocean Wave, and the Giant Racer.

And they came to see him, the Lionman, tamed King of Beasts, reclining on a pile of Turkey carpets. The brave and entitled demanded locks of his long, coarse mane as if they were talismans or trophies. He'd seen photos of rich men leaning on long rifles beside lion, rhino, and elephant carcasses, had been chased by poor men holding rocks, shouting epithets. A clipping seemed a small price for his ease of mind. He back-flipped three or four times in a row across the stage for a fist of coins, more for the pleasure and rush of movement, even though his knees and shoulders ached after a lifetime of acrobatics. One day, he'd miss and break his leg or crack his skull. Who would pay to see him then, hobbling on crutches, head wrapped like a mummy?

When the park emptied of the teeming crowds and fell quiet except for the odd roadster trundling down Surf Avenue, or the muted trumpets of Little Hip, the elephant, or the pickled laughter of other freaks staggering by (as much as it was possible to stagger with no legs or four), the Lionman stood at the window of the Baby Incubators, a mock farmhouse with timber beams and a gabled roof, better suited for Yorkshire than Brooklyn. Anchored at the peak, a stone stork hovered over a nest of cherubs, its beak pointed as if at a trough of herring. Inside the building, there was a row of premature infants in the incubators, boys pinned with blue ribbons, girls with pink. The heated boxes more peanut roasters than scientific wonders. Sometimes a nurse, the hefty one, eased an infant's arm from the swaddling and slipped her diamond ring over the tiny fingers, then hand, making an impromptu Tiffany bangle. Women tugged off their own rings, held them between their fingers, estimating the impossible measurement.

He pressed against the Baby Incubators window, hair tickling his face like a woman's lips might, though this was an approximate feeling as even prostitutes, granting a fuck, refused such intimacies. They did allow him, for fifty cents, to palm their pocked cheeks and trace the fine down from their temples to jaws. Afterward, he stood at the sink, washing the tacky residue of face paint from his hands, and stared into the dim, spidered mirror, trying to see past his given lot. Dark eyes visible, but the planes of his face? A self obscured beneath hair, fur, coat, pelt? Time moving forward and through him, evidenced by the occasional silver strands plucked from his forehead and chin, but otherwise the same. He could only, always, look away.

Years before, the Lionman traveled in Baron Von Hausmann's circus across the continent. The baron was a tall, rickety man, his imperial mustache an autocratic punctuation. He locked the Lionman inside a small, rusty cage once home to a screeching monkey that served tea to a filthy doll; it died after drinking from a bucket of green paint. The Lionman, still a boy, was ordered to leap and growl at the bars, at little girls in particular, though they often giggled at his exaggerated, high-pitched ferocity. By evening, invariably tired and hungry, he slumped to the ground. The baron whacked the bars with his cane, jabbing his ribs, startling him awake.

Once, he woke to a woman's gloved finger stroking the long hair on his cheek. An exquisite tenderness, filled with pity and yearning. He shivered, mesmerized in sensation. She perched beside his cage, her black taffeta skirt collapsed around her in gleaming folds—a crow waiting clear-eyed on the tip of a branch. A toque cantilevered on top of a loose coil of hair. He held her steady blue eyes with his, waiting for her scream, for the chicken bone thrown from a pocket. This was what people did—shouted and threw scraps of food. In the countryside anyway, when the tents were set up in muddy fields ripe with horse shit. In the city, less food and more coins were tossed through the bars.

The woman was close, her shallow inhalations and exhalations audible, and then so quick it might never have happened at all, her face was against the rusty bars, her fingertips were beneath his chin, and lips were on his.

"*Mein liebes Kind,*" she said, a whispered, sorrowful secret. An iron flake, a rusty petal, stuck to her creamy cheek; he imagined her whole face in bloom, tipped to the sun. Reach through the bars and brush it away? Disastrous. The baron had beaten him for less.

Her hand rustled in her dress and reappeared, bills pinched between her fingers. She flicked them angrily, and they scattered on the straw-covered ground. Had the strange yoking of sympathy and desire cost her too much? She rose, her back dismissing him. No matter. He had her money. Paper easier to hide than coins in the slit seam of his thin mattress. He lurched and snarled as she disappeared into the crowd.

The incubator infants were swaddled in white blankets, wrapped tight against the shadows. So small and their need so great. Weeks and weeks early for this world. No defenses except the metal and glass boxes (what a magician might escape from in seconds), and Dr. Couney with his charts, droppers, and needles, and the wet nurses whisking them to the nutrition parlor in back. Warm air, regulated by a thermostat, pumped through pipes across the bottoms of the incubators. Nothing more, really, than heated water chambers at a chick hatchery. The narrow mattresses rested on scales monitoring weight to the tenth of a gram: 970g, 1120g, 1460g—large black numbers on cards attached to the boxes. Twice a day, the nurses switched the cards out, their faces flat and impassive as they took the readings. Spectators sneezed into grubby handkerchiefs, breathed their germy breath, and reached over the railing, leaving greasy fingerprints on the incubators' windows. The nurses, in their spotless white dresses and peaked caps, strode through with rags and Lysol bottles, rubbed at the glass in brisk, determined circles, then shoed back the crowds to wipe the railings.

The Lionman noted all this during his breaks each day and at night, when he was free to walk unmolested. He watched the nurse, the one with the soft eyes and hair that shimmered yellow like the fields in Bavaria. The sun there had fallen in benediction across wheat as it spread out from the train tracks. His head had bumped a rhythm against the compartment's window. He imagined vaulting from the train like the Indian acrobats from their ladders, his mane, which he combed for fleas, lice, and chaff, disheveled from the flight and tumble. If he kept his bare palms and soles to the ground, he could disappear into all that rolling light.

Hildegard.

Violetta, the Half-Woman, told him her name. Dr. Couney called his daughter Hildy, and the two promenaded around the park in the evening like mismatched sweethearts. The doctor was always impeccable in dark broadcloth, spats, and a derby; he stooped, though, leaning on a crooked cane, and grasped his daughter's arm as they walked past the exhibits, lingering at the entrances. He talked, gestured, and talked more, perhaps agitated by the day's events in the nursery; she listened, nodded, and steered him through the crowd. In contrast to her father, Hildegard stood tall, her shoulders thrust back in youthful assurance and enthusiasm. It must have required great restraint to keep to her father's measured pace; on her solitary walks, her feet moved quickly beneath her skirts and her arms switched back and forth, a purely constitutional outing.

The Lionman had been lying beside Violetta, a usual consideration to mitigate the distance between them since, like half a dress form, she had no arms or legs; of course, using her teeth, she sewed her armless dresses, lit cigarettes, and sketched spectators. And sang, not especially well, but with bravado—what it took when you looked like them. Sea shanties she learned from Ajax, the Sword Swallower: "The Saucy Sailor Boy," "Whiskey Johnny," and "New York Girls." He propped his head with his hand; the kinky waves of his mane brushed the ground. He was still in costume: red Ottoman vest embroidered with gold flowers, blue, silk sash knotted at the waist, and black pantaloons.

"You're a pasha," Violetta said, nudging him with her hip, a side shuffle she'd perfected. "You need a harem of those ticket girls."

Those girls wore blue academic robes and mortarboards and stood in their booths, selling wheels of tickets each day. At night, as the lights flickered out across the park, the girls gathered at the entrance beside the massive, gold columns, then left in tight clusters for the train, glancing warily at the freaks ending their own long days in raucous, liquored companionship.

He smiled, lips closed over his nine teeth, all he had ever had.

Violetta puffed her cigarette. "Imagine fucking one of them! And that girl, Couney's daughter. You know, she was one of us, in one of those incubators. A regular miracle." She spat the end of her cigarette to the ground where it glowed, then winked out.

"We all are," he said, "surviving them." *Them*, the unmaimed who gawked and jeered, grabbed and punched and worse. When Violetta was a girl, a drunk carried her under his arm to an alley where he had his way, then left her with the garbage and rats, and her torn undergarments thrown, she joked, just out of reach. Violetta recounted this one night as they talked of their time in the Chicago Exhibition where the Lionman had held her on his lap on the Ferris wheel, the world's first, as it rose up and down, carrying two thousand people above the dazzling white buildings, high enough to see the endless lake, and the distant city stretch out before them. They boasted of the indignities they'd suffered, trading pain like the coin of the realm. Worse to be a Lionman or a Sealman? Nine feet or eighteen inches? Siamese twin or no limbs?

In the late afternoons, Hildegard stood in the building's shade, drinking a glass of water in long generous sips, throat moving with each swallow. She untied her apron, lifted it over her head, and shook it three times. The fabric crackled in the air. She took off her cap, holding the pins between her lips, and her hair tumbled down her back in a glossy wave. She gathered it to one side, wiped her hand across her neck, and in one easy motion, twisted her hair and tucked it away.

Once a freak. He tongued the gaps in his mouth. Part of his ailment. What the physicians in Gdańsk, Rome, and Manhattan called Owłosienie nadmierne, politricosi, *hyper-trichosis*. The words meant nothing since there was no cure. Skeins of hair and teeth in ruins. Except for mercenary interests, none of *them* came near him. During his passage on the Hamburg-American, he remained for all six days in his steerage cabin, eating the bruised apples, stale bread, and hard-boiled eggs he had wrapped in a wool scarf. His cabin mate refused to share the room and so he was alone, passing the hours in anxious sleep or rereading a copy of *Scientific American* he'd found on a trolley in the hall—a new spindle for spinning wool, a turbine waterwheel, a bull with two mouths. Men knocked on his door, jiggled the knob, shouted for him to show his face, but he stayed out of sight, behind the lock, the only guarantee some drunk, who once he saw his face, wouldn't toss him overboard. In the deep hours of night, he staggered down the passageway to use the toilet, the ship pitching and rolling, slamming him against walls; during the day, he pissed and heaved into the refuse bin.

One morning, before the park opened, he and Mortado, the Human Fountain, watched Captain Jack work Black Prince, the lion, in the arena. The trainer and lion were in a cage bigger than his own in the baron's circus, big enough for the animal to run—when prodded by the whip—in a wide circle, its muscles rippling beneath its sandy coat. Captain Jack fed it meat from a bucket outside the bars; he wiped the blood from his hands on a towel, then rubbed the lion's neck, his fingers disappearing into the shaggy, black mane. The lion's attention never wavered; it sat up on hind legs over and over, without protest or antagonism, the repetition erasing instinct. But then, it had never raced across the savannah pursuing an antelope or slept in the dust in the blasted heat, tasseled tail twitching at flies. Instead, it only knew cages and railcars and wheelbarrows of bones and butchered horse meat.

"If there was anything else you could do?" Mortado asked. He poked the corks from the holes bored through his palms and feet, and began cleaning the wounds, a meticulous, daily necessity to keep infection at bay. For his act, copper tubes snaked through the holes and spurted water at the audience. On Saturdays, he reenacted the crucifixion, stuffing pouches of red fluid in the holes; an assistant, dressed as a soldier of the Roman Legion, drove in the nails. One of the most successful acts. People fainted.

"What would I be? A dentist?" the Lionman asked. And not because in that life, he might have most of his teeth, but because people would tremble at him for this reason alone, and it would be in his power to soothe them in Polish, Russian, German, or English, any of the languages he knew, he would have the words to quiet their fear, the skills to help them and the tools to see it through—picks, pliers, morphine. *Dies wird nicht wehtun.* (This won't hurt). When he sat on his pile of Turkey carpets, he spoke to the crowd, softly, to bring them close, but they couldn't hear him for his fearsome strangeness. *Ich werde dir nicht wehtun.* (I won't hurt you). "I wouldn't choose this life. But you," the Lionman said, "you do this to yourself. The money isn't that good."

Mortado shrugged, poured water in his palm; it splashed through to the ground. "Even if it's a con? I'm astonishing. People come to see me. If I was a bookkeeper, a shoeshiner, a deliveryman? Every week, I survive what Jesus Christ himself could not."

The Lionman did not think of himself as astonishing. An overgrown curiosity, occasionally terrifying the very young, but he had no fangs, was nothing to run away from. Like Black Prince, cowed by the whip and chair, by the captain, a man of ordinary size and strength. But then last week, he lion swiped the captain's hand with its claw, hooking tendon and bone. Despite amputation, Captain Jack died from infection. Black Prince, freed from the tricks, now circled its pen without purpose or audience. The Lionman walked by the cage before his own performance one morning. The lion paced the bars, pausing before changing direction. Time enough to imagine something else, some inherited idea of open sky and space? Could he slip his hand through the bars and stroke its neck, the sinew and muscle tightening beneath him, contact the lion must long for, or certainly miss, or at least register its absence? But he wasn't kin, and the lion would just as surely spear his hand or neck.

"You're here again." Hildegard stood under the lamp, a beetle thumping against the bulb. A statement, not a question: he was an obvious presence, usually surrounded by children pointing and shrieking and tugging at his mane. The reason for coming at night.

"Dreamland is Dreamland," he said. "Gondolas float under the Rialto, pass the Doge's Palace, and Pompeii forever erupts, the city and its people always buried under ash," he said. "History is tedious. One thing after another without change."

She laughed, but her eyes remained cool and level, appraising him. "The nurses are afraid of you. It's silly, but they insist the infants' hearts quicken when you're near."

"They're the true Lilliputians," he said. "Only they grow and their parents return and they leave. Easy happiness in all that possibility." He stepped closer; she smelled clean, the tar of carbolic soap, in comparison to his musk. At times, his animal self was undeniable. The day had been hot and the air under the red, velvet curtains heavy and stagnant. His underarms and crotch were spongy and slick with sweat.

"Some die," she said. "Parents leave with another box which they bury in the ground. Most of the visitors who scrap together ten cents are mothers, or were. Their longing is terrible. They fall to the ground, climb over the railings, get tangled up in their skirts, and are hauled off by guards."

"They're wanted," he said, smiling, lips tight against the jumble in his mouth. He didn't say this to gain easy sympathy, merely to state what it meant to earn a living from disease, misfortune, or deliberate mutilation. And to acknowledge his own desire, what held him to the window night after night. As Violetta said: the premature infants were freaks, the incubator building on their side of the park. But they would become more than their beginning condition. No seal fins, no scales, and unlike Princess Wee Wee, taller than twenty-four inches.

"I'm Hildegard," she said and held out her hand.

He took his time reaching out, extending the moment. So few physical intimacies, and always a shock. He'd been denied a routine erotic life, substituting small sensual pleasures—an apple peel unwinding between his thumb and pocketknife; a comb pulling down his neck, then chest, and arms, the teeth surprising and sharp on his bare palms. Cold water rising up his shins, lapping his thighs as he waded into the surf.

Hildegard's hand was sturdy and rough—all that scrubbing—and her fingers tightened around his, without hesitation or feminine deference. He wanted to kiss her hand in gallant daring, but feared she would tug away, offended.

"I'm the Lionman."

"Yes," she said, "but your name?"

Ordinary, which made it ridiculous as he had never been who he was born to be. "Stephan. Stephan Bibrowski." A name rarely used, except to sign for wages.

"Stephan, come with me." She turned and walked into the building. Her skirts whirled around her ankles.

The other nurse, Rausch, resisted. She stood in the aisle, ready to push them back. The room was lit only by dim sconces, and quiet, no crowds, just the infants asleep, a kind of hibernation in their dens, dreaming…of nothing, because what have they experienced from which dreams could expand and shift and terrify and delight? What alternative could their dreams offer? The Lionman woke from his own dreams panicked, heart racing, gulping for air, wondering where he was even though, of course, he was in his rented room with the creaky bedsprings and the chipped green bowl and pitcher. Even so, he felt heckled and pursued in dreams rather than freed from his life.

"No," Nurse Rausch said. "Against protocol." Everything about her was efficient and disciplined: dark hair pulled into a solid bun; Oxfords gleamed with polish; eyes fixed on Hildegard, refusing to see him.

Hildegard shrugged. "My father will fire me?"

The woman took a wider stance. "He will infect them with disease."

The Lionman turned over his hands; and while they couldn't see his clean palms, they could see they were smooth.

Hildegard bumped past her. "He can wash in the back."

At the sink, she turned on the faucet and gave him the cake of red soap. "Scrub hard," she said, scissoring palms in demonstration. The hair on the backs of his hands lathered into wet, stringy clumps like seaweed along a shore. He rinsed and shook off the water.

"Here. Hold them out." Hildegard folded a white towel around his hands and rubbed, as if drying a boy's sopping head. Difficult to hold steady. She dropped the towel into a bin, then poured a capful of antiseptic into his hands. "Now rub again," she said without sentiment. And then a grin. "Safeguard. No lice." Her teeth were crooked on the bottom, a charming imperfection.

He didn't remember much of his own mother. She had sold him to the Baron when he was five. Mostly, he recalled her screaming through his bedroom door that he was an abomination, her voice strained, then splitting apart into tears. He would put his eye to the keyhole: blue fabric covered in white polka dots, a wedge of pink knuckle, then her dark eye pinned to his. She was quiet; he held his breath and imagined his mother might finally see him, see into him, without the distraction of his offending body. She could hold him like this in her gaze; he asked for nothing more. But then he blinked, and she was gone, clunking back down the stairs in her brown boots that were tied with lengths of butcher's string knotted together.

What she told the doctors she consulted: when she was pregnant, his father was mauled to death by the mangy lion at the city zoo. She was there, had seen it happen. The stupid man, she said, had dropped his gold pocket watch, a gift from a rich uncle when he entered university, into the walled pit. The lion, asleep at the back, indolent from the heat, was at first unaware of her husband's descent down the access ladder, despite the large sign that read: "Keep Out." But then it charged: one heavy paw to the neck, and her husband was dead. When Stephan was born two months later, slick and covered with hair, she knew her infant was cursed, and refused to hold him to her breast. Even the wet nurse was paid double. "Better you should have shriveled up," she hissed at him in later years, when he pleaded hunger or thirst.

His mother made attempts, shaving him each day, sometimes twice a day. But how could she bring him outside, covered in all those scabby nicks? She had an unsteady hand since she'd taken to brandy. Besides, neighbors and shopkeepers were afraid, whispered that he was a werewolf. Better to lock him in his bedroom, change out the slop bucket, and go on with her life. Once a week, she brought him to the kitchen to stand in a tub of icy water, the gas lamp hissing in the corner, and though it sounded malevolent, the lamp cast his haggard mother in a warm glow. So that while she was scouring him with the rough sponge, he understood that this might be as close to love as he would ever get.

Hildegard draped a sheet across him at the insistent suggestion of Nurse Rausch, who stood by the door, unforgiving in her disapproval. Even in the half-light, the immense diamond sparkled on her stout finger; neither a utilitarian nor straight-forward ornament, yet proof of extravagant desire.

She caught his glance, slipped off the ring, and put it in her pocket. "Paste," she said. "Part of the show. The doctor's idea to use it for demonstration on the infants."

Hildegard opened an incubator's door. Warm, humid air drifted out. Boggy, like moss, but talcum powder, too. A pink ribbon was pinned over the baby's cap. Hildegard stroked the satin strip.

"Her heart isn't much bigger than your thumbnail," she said. "But it's enough."

He looked down at his uneven nails and ragged cuticles, the white half-moons hidden by a fringe of hair. Surely Rausch was correct in her assessment. The child should be left in its warming pan, undisturbed, untroubled. But Hildegard was already lifting her out of the incubator and into his arms, a potential world of harm. He'd never held an infant. A puppy, a kitten, even a tiger cub once whose razor claws raked through his own ten inches of fur, then skin, hair drying in a bloody clump. The child weighed less than his curled leather slippers, but still so easy to drop. Her face was smooth and untroubled, without history. Only a wisp of hair whorled on top of her head.

What he longed for was in the infant's face: no suffering, no shame. Was his pain worth it? A bottle of morphine, wrapped in a sock in the back corner of a bureau drawer, answered to that. An ever-ready alternative. If she lived, the infant would live an ordinary life. A pram, a frilly blanket tucked around her, the autumn sun flashing across her face. The family cat, waving its tail just out of reach, a tantrum when it darted off. A schoolyard, a game of tag, a spelling test.

Hildegard looked at the chart on the incubator. "Four weeks and still losing weight." She deflated.

What should he say? That he would, against reason, knowing nothing about the infant or the parents, of their circumstances, rich or poor, or their composition, generous or mean, give his life for hers? He had always been aware, to the penny, of what his life was worth. He had made peace with longing, knew how much to pay for a fuck since it never came free from reciprocal desire, knew circumstances might alter exterior space—city, apartment, stage show—but the interior space—solitary—would remain unchanged. He would never be a father; even a prostitute, if accidentally with his child, would panic and demand a knitting needle. But to claim something, someone, as his own other than what he could fit inside a steamer trunk or pocket or sock. To be held in place by another's needs. To be what is needed.

The infant's body moved with each slight breath; her heat settled into him. As he studied her small face, he saw, as if rising out of relief, that she had no brows or lashes. Unsettling. And her red skin, mapped with blue veins, was covered in fuzz.

"This hair?" He couldn't finish. Was this how he had presented to the world?

"Most are covered in it," Hildegard said. She reached over and touched the baby's forehead, riffling the tiny hairs. "In a few weeks, it will fall out and then nothing between her and the world."

"Maybe with all this hair, I'm too early, too" he said.

She laughed. "The incubators are effective but not enough."

"You can get used to anything," he said, and in an imperceptible but brutal movement, shifted the infant away from him. A careful cradle without connection, like holding a stunned fish or balancing a tray of champagne flutes. He wondered at the size of his own heart, a tight fist, and under what circumstances it might open.

Hildegard fiddled with a button on her cuff, pushing it in and out of the buttonhole. "You could come when I'm here, at night. You could help," she said.

Night after night, expectation and fulfillment. Such an arrangement would never last.

Hildegard buttoned her cuff and busied herself with temperatures and weights and diapers. On the infant's chart, a name: Martha Lloyd. Her eyes blinked open, and she seemed to look up at him and he looked down at her and wondered: who will you be, if you live, Martha Lloyd? Likely, the infant only saw an indiscriminate shadow.

A startling, discordant clanging. The fire alarm. All the park's fire alarms. The Lionman clutched the infant to him, instinct perhaps, though he would have held a dog just the same. Both nurses rushed to the windows. Outside, beyond Lilliputia, Hell Gate was on fire. Flames already engulfed the roof and the enormous winged demon that hunched over the eaves. Sparks lifted by the updraft landed around Baby Incubators like cannon fire. The building would burn and they would die if they stayed.

Hildegard and Nurse Rausch shouted at him as they unlatched the incubators.

He could with certainty hold four.

Their walk across Dreamland for Luna Park was a mostly silent, grim procession. The world was on fire: orange flames and billowing, dark smoke consumed the Baby Incubators, the power plant, the White Tower, Shoot-the-Chutes, and the Destruction of Babylon. Steam engines and hook-and-ladders, already too late, sounded a continual alarm. Firemen fought with leather hoses that pulsed sporadic water from failing pumps. Hell's Gate and all fifty acres of buildings, constructed of lath and staff, like plaster of Paris models, collapsed. Lightbulbs popped overhead, raining slivers of glass. Shells exploded in the shooting gallery as if war had commenced. In the arena, animals growled and screeched.

Hildegard held two infants in one arm; with her free hand, she flicked cinders off her dress. The Lionman ignored the welts on his body and singed hair—it would grow back, it always did; otherwise, he would have bathed in flames long ago. He carried two infants in each arm; Hildegard and Nurse Rausch each held three cradled in their aprons, the way children might gather up wild berries in their shirts. They stopped often, rearranging the blankets over the infants' faces and feeling for their breath. He might as well have been checking the life signs of sparrows, but *Yes*, he said, *I feel them all*. And then: Violetta. Did someone carry her out, or was she waiting like the last bowling pin in the lane? Surely, she had been sitting with the rest in the hall, cards in hand, bets and whisky on the table, laughing over idiots who asked whether they had cock traps and bum balls, hearts and brains, whether they were humans at all.

How close to hold the infants? How quickly, but carefully to step? The parents, oblivious, asleep in their beds in Manhattan or Astoria or Flushing, curtains pulled, empty crib assembled in such great, sad hope. If he tripped? Under his weight, the infants would smash like eggs.

Hildegard was sure-footed despite her skirts. "People must think you stole off with dinner," she said. No one looked twice.

When they reached the Baby Incubators at Luna Park, nurses, without thanks or a second looks, took the infants from him and threw the sooty blankets in the trash bin. He'd only seen the infants bundled up, layer upon layer, heads capped, little Eskimos ready for the fierce, inhospitable cold. But now, lying on the steel examination tables, they resembled newborn rabbits, skin mottled red and purple and covered in fine hair. They mewled when the nurses trickled water over their bodies, washed them with their fingertips, and rubbed them dry.

Hildegard was busy; her father had arrived and she dashed about under his orders, forgetting the Lionman, as it should be; he never assumed Hildegard held anything but kind, circumstantial regard for him as a fixture of Dreamland, a curiosity. But he stood outside and watched the flames bleed into the dark sky, and Hildegard scribbling on charts, and the infants who would leave one day for those empty cribs, or would not, but who would never remember any of this. Not Dreamland, not Dr. Couney or Hildegard, not the lion who held them.

He listened to stories from Dreamland's wandering survivors. About how the bear cub, the one that rode the bicycle, was found on Surf Avenue, the tips of its ears melted and eyes swollen shut. About how the animals in the arena had been loose, the trainers herding them in a procession to wait out the chaos of the fire, but the lights went out and the panicked animals turned on each other as the walls collapsed. About how Black Prince charged from the arena, mane a burning halo. Police shot him in the train tunnels; an officer split his skull with an ax. Onlookers fought over souvenirs—chopped the tail, hacked the mane, broke off teeth.

He waited just as he had waited at his bedroom door for his mother to stagger up the stairs, his eye to the keyhole, plucking hair after hair from his body in hopes that she might stay. And when he tired of waiting? While watching Dreamland's end, he might understand his own: ordinary. An apartment in Berlin on the top floor so the curtains could stay open and the light fall in. The grocery boy would knock with the delivery—eggs, bread, and apples—but no answer. Day after day. And then the smell. The constable would be summoned. In the bathroom, they would find the tub filled with water, now cold, the soap under the toilet, and the Lionman on the floor, but not naked, not with all that silver hair.

Acknowledgments

I am immensely grateful to my family and friends whose love and forbearance keeps me equally grounded and inspired. Thanks to my agent, Anne Borchardt, and The Georges Borchardt Agency for supporting my work for these many years. And to the generous editorial staff at Braddock Avenue Books, particularly Jeffrey Condran and Robert Peluso, my thanks for bringing this book into the world. Writing these stories meant that my words mattered, if only to me, and in no small part, the writing is what kept me here and able to offer these thanks. Wonder words, indeed.

Kerry Neville was raised on Long Island, New York and now lives in Georgia where she teaches at Georgia College and State University. Her first collection of stories, *Necessary Lies*, received the G.S. Sharat Chandra Prize in Fiction and was named a *ForeWord Magazine* Short Story Book of the Year. Her work has appeared in various journals, including *The Gettysburg Review*, *Epoch*, and *Triquarterly*, and online in publications such as *The Washington Post*, *The Huffington Post*, and *The Fix*. She has twice been the recipient of the Dallas Museum of Art's "Arts and Letters Prize for Fiction," and has also been awarded the Texas Institute of Letters Kay Cattarulla Prize for the Short Story and the John Guyon Literary Nonfiction Prize from *Crab Orchard Review*.

Photo credit: Kerry Brown